# THE LOST LOVE LIAISON

## A LORA WEAVER MYSTERY NOVELLA

### KATY LEEN

ISBN: Print: 978-0-9936165-6-3

Cover design: Team KL

Cover illustration by Adrienne Alexander

Cover background icons: The Noun Project, heart #8181231

*For my mother, who could always find joy in ordinary things and fill ordinary things with joy.*

_V_ ALENTINE'S DAY IS supposed to be for romance not roaming. That's why it's so suited to February. When the winter cold adds extra incentive to hibernate at home and cuddle, instead of venturing out looking for trouble.

This was especially true in Montreal this year when snow still fell three days out of seven and it was colder than the ice cream waiting for me in my freezer at home. The ice cream I could be feasting on at this very moment if Mélanie Gauthier hadn't hired the PI agency I worked for to shadow her husband, Martin Single-ton, and find out who was getting all the attention he used to bestow on Mélanie and their two kids.

Apparently, Martin wasn't hibernating at home like he should be. Martin was thumbing his nose at the cold and roaming far and wide to find his trouble. That's how I got stuck spending my Valentine's in Sainte-Adèle, about 85 kilometers from the city, sans boyfriend, dining in a ski resort restaurant that had a view of a mountain to my right and to my left, a view of Martin Singleton and a woman I was guessing was his new lady friend.

I leaned down, pretending to get something from the purse I'd set on the floor beside my chair, and I risked a look at Martin, sitting three tables away, in the darkest corner of the restaurant. He was fortyish, slim, and decked out in a tailored gray suit over a patterned blue shirt, tie loose at his neck, brown hair cut tidy and trimmed around his ears. His focus held steady on the woman sitting with him, at least ten years his junior. A redhead with cascades of curls, freckled cheeks, and sparkly eye shadow. She wore a red pencil skirt fitted to slope in at her tiny waist and a crisp white blouse buttoned barely high enough to conceal her bra.

"What is this guy thinking?" I murmured to myself as I sat up and went back to hiding behind my menu. "Nobody cheats on Valentine's day."

Warm fingers slid over my hands and gently directed them downwards, menu and all, and infiltrating eyes bore into mine. Dark eyes set off by wild dark hair and dark scruff. Eyes that left me feeling like I'd forgotten to dress. Eyes that belonged to my boss, Laurent Caron—ex-cop, ex-hockey leaguer, and expert investigator.

"*Vraiment*, Lora. In your fairy tale world does anyone ever cheat?" he said, his usual throaty, French accent made deeper by his hushed tone.

I eased my hands out of his and moved my menu back up to camouflage height, my eyes peeking out just enough to keep watch on Martin. "I don't live in a fairy tale world," I told Laurent. Although I had to admit, it had felt a bit like it lately. After all, I had moved from New York to Montreal to live with my boyfriend Adam, my very own Prince Charming. And I was living in a beautiful house made of sturdy bricks the big bad wolf could never blow down. And I was granted my wish of starting a new career as a PI, well PI in training. A job I loved even more than my old one as a social worker.

Too bad Mélanie Gauthier wasn't having the same luck as I was. I grimaced on her behalf as I spotted Martin playing footsie under the table with his lady friend, her stockinged foot making its way up past his ankle and disappearing into his pant leg.

"But fair is fair," I went on to say. "If a relationship's over, fine, couples should move on. But they should pack it in first before anyone starts storing their goods in someone else's boxes."

Laurent smiled at me across our table and leaned forward, lowering his voice even more. "Maybe we should wait to have evidence before we decide where Monsieur Martin Singleton is storing his goods, no?"

Laurent was right, of course. We didn't have actual proof of any wrongdoing. And maybe I was wrong about Martin. Maybe he was totally on the up and up. Maybe the redhead would turn out to be an old friend. A friend who played footsie with Martin for old time's sake, like it was hopscotch.

After all, appearances could be deceiving. If my boyfriend Adam saw me now for instance, spending the dinner hour with Laurent in a posh restaurant in a swanky resort with ski hills, fine food, and roaring fires everywhere I looked, he may not have been so understanding about postponing our own Valentine's night until after I got off work. Adam had been jealous enough when I'd pretended to be Laurent's fiancée on a previous case. He would not be happy to know I was passing the better part of the most romantic day of the year once again pretending to be hooked to Laurent. Probably it wouldn't soothe Adam much to know at least I wasn't faux engaged this time.

And it didn't soothe me, either. I wasn't so thrilled about spending Valentine's working the night shift. I was itching to leave. I had added a few extra waves to my auburn mane of hair and a dash of mascara to my blue eyes. And I was already wearing the pink, slinky dress I'd bought especially for the occasion, with matching kitten-heeled shoes that lengthened my legs and added almost two inches to all five foot two of me. I even had my gift for Adam tucked away in my handbag. The minute we were done here, I was ready to hightail it back to the city to be with my Valentine. I had no plans to leave Adam all alone like Martin Singleton was doing to poor Mélanie Gauthier.

I glanced back at Martin and watched as he slowly slid locks of his companion's hair from her bosom to her shoulders, then sat back, held up his phone, and took a picture of her. She smiled, her cheeks growing rounder, and it took me a moment to realize there was something different about her from the last time I'd looked over. Her cleavage now nestled a gold necklace weighed down by a hefty emerald.

"You don't think that's evidence?" I whispered to Laurent. "The guy just gave her a stone pricey enough to cover a down payment on a car, and now they're all over each other."

To underscore my second point, my eyes darted to the current liplock connecting Martin to the redhead, and Laurent turned his head to follow my eyes then set his gaze back on me. "Surely, Lora, you don't mean that kiss? An innocent kiss between friends maybe. Nothing wrong with that. Even *you* would have to agree one little kiss is not cheating." He raised an eyebrow on that last bit, nearly daring me to disagree.

I couldn't of course. I knew he was baiting me. Not so long ago, the two of us had shared a kiss. Purely in the line of work, on the undercover case when we'd been pretend engaged. And the kiss was completely harmless. So harmless, I'd almost forgotten about the feel of Laurent's lips on mine, the taste of wine on his breath, the grip of his strong hands on my back. And I'd do an even better job of forgetting if he'd stop bringing it up to tease me.

I lowered my menu. "That kiss was completely different and you know it," I said. "That was work."

He shrugged in that way that only the French can. "Maybe Martin is at work, too."

"As what? A tonsil inspector?"

Truth was, I hated working infidelity cases. I would have loved to believe Martin Singleton was innocent so we could go back to Mélanie Gauthier and assure her that her suspicions were for naught and her marriage was hunky dory. But if Martin was guilty, Mélanie deserved to know. At least then she'd know her instincts were spot on and she wasn't imagining things.

Our waitress came over—college age, streaked blonde hair worn up in a messy bun, cute dimple in one cheek when she smiled. She deposited drinks and appetizers on our table then lingered, coyly tapping her pen, and asked Laurent in French if there was anything else she could get for him. Not us, but him. I got nothing but a cold stare as she left. I got that a lot from women when I was with Laurent. Especially when we were posing as a couple. Some women seemed to resent the idea of another woman taking Laurent off the market before they'd had their chance to sample the goods. Probably it didn't help that he currently wore a suit that likely debuted on an Italian runway. Or that it formed to his toned body, advertising his good genes and good workout regime. Not to mention that Laurent and I were on the set of romance central, sitting at a table complete with fine white linen, sparkling dinnerware, crystal goblets, two lit candles, a single red rose cloaked in a glass jar, and a giant chocolate cupid—naked except for a red candy crown of flowers on his head.

When the waitress had cleared earshot, Laurent slid the candles aside and filled our glasses from the bottle the waitress had left in a standing canister lined with ice.

I brought my glass up to my nose and took a whiff. "Is that champagne?"

Laurent nodded. "*Évidement*. It's better for our cover, no?"

I sat back and eyed the hors d'oeuvres the waitress had brought. Lots of vegetables sculpted into hearts along with some crackers and cheese.

I skimmed the tables around me for onlookers, sure now that if they'd known I had a boyfriend, I wouldn't look any better than Martin Singleton. Maybe Laurent was right. Maybe I was jumping to conclusions about Martin.

I checked in with Martin again. This time, he was passing his dinner companion a gift bag decorated with white hearts on a red background, loads of gold ribbon attached to the bag's handles. She smiled and let out a slight laugh as she pulled out the contents, something black and lacy that looked like moths had gotten to it and that disappeared back into the bag faster than it had been fished out.

Okay, that didn't look good. At least Laurent wasn't passing me any gift bags with hearts. I reached for a cracker and popped it in my mouth, which is when I noticed the small pink box set in front of me. A box with a tiny silver bow on top.

I raised my eyes to meet Laurent's. "For me?" I asked him, caught off guard, my voice dipping.

He waggled his eyebrows at me. "I think we have seen enough of Martin Singleton. You open your gift now."

I grabbed my champagne glass and took a swig then stared down at the box. I had to open it, right? It would be rude to just ignore it. I guzzled the rest of my champagne and took the lid off the box. Inside was a beautiful vintage key. A hotel key to be exact, for a room upstairs.

I looked up, about to ask Laurent what he was thinking giving me the key, only to see my boyfriend Adam standing three feet away. The look on his face and the fisted hand by his side telling me he was probably about to ask Laurent the same question.

# 2

---

"THERE YOU ARE," Adam said, mouth tight, eyes shifting from me to Laurent then to me again. His short brown hair was damp in places, the scent of fresh snow wafting from his head. His tall, lean body was clothed in an immaculate black suit set off by a linen shirt open at the collar. No overcoat in sight.

"*Oui*. Here she is," Laurent said, standing and pushing his chair back. He adjusted his shirt cuffs and stepped to the side of the table.

Adam moved towards Laurent's chair. "I thought Camille was bringing her."

"Camille was busy with her chum," Laurent said.

Camille was my best friend and Laurent's sister. Also joint owner of the investigative agency where I worked, C&C, which made her my other boss. And Laurent was right. She had Valentine plans for the evening with the current beau in her life, Paul Bell aka Puddles, a man she'd met on a case a couple months earlier who had slithered into her bed and stayed there. Normally,

Camille shed men the way snakes shed skin, so time would tell how long their coiling would last. Probably Puddles had lured Camille into celebrating Valentine's with promises of vast amounts of chocolate and few requests for commitment.

At the moment, I was less curious about that and more curious about what these guys were talking about. Which must have shown on my face because Laurent said, "A very lovely Valentine's day to you, Lora. I leave you now to Adam."

It was strange hearing Laurent say Adam instead of calling him my Anglophone like he did when we were alone. It took me a split second to follow what he was saying. "So we're done with the case for tonight?" I said.

Laurent smiled. "There is no case. That was a ruse."

I looked from him to Adam. "What do you mean? What about Mélanie Gauthier?"

Laurent drifted closer to me. "She is happy and well and sitting over there with her husband, Martin. She is a childhood friend of Camille and me, from our *quartier*. Martin and Mélanie come to Sainte-Adèle every year for *Saint-Valentin*, the *anniversaire* of their wedding here." He turned his smile towards Martin's table and gave a little wave. Both Martin and the redhead waved back.

Adam sat in Laurent's chair, dropped a valet slip from his fisted hand, and raised the glass of champagne in front of him. The glass I realized Laurent had never touched. Adam tipped the glass at me. "Happy Valentine's day, hon. I wanted to surprise you. Take you somewhere nice without you suspecting a thing. Camille agreed to help and set this up. She even chose the place." He worked his mouth into a polite smile and tipped the glass in Laurent's direction. "Thanks, man, for stepping in for her and making sure Lora got here."

Laurent nodded acknowledgement and Adam shifted his raised glass back to me, reaching forward halfway across the table.

I scrambled to raise my glass to meet his, only my glass was empty. Not that I had to look inside the glass to see that, I could tell by the slight buzz settling in my head. I was a lightweight drinker—one glass of anything and I was tipsy, two glasses and I was on my way to LaLa land.

Adam clinked my empty glass and took a sip of his champagne, so I feigned doing the same then stood when I noticed Laurent walking away. "You leaving?" I said to him.

He turned and smiled, eyes crinkling at the sides. He stepped back to the champagne stand, pulled out the bottle, and refilled my glass. "I'll see you at work the day after tomorrow," he said by way of answer. He slipped behind me and settled me and my chair back at the table. "*Amuse-toi bien.*" And he left, stopping briefly at Martin and Mélanie's table on his way out.

I watched Laurent go then my eyes darted again to Martin and Mélanie as I processed the twist in the evening's agenda. They were both laughing quietly, their cheeks rosy in the candlelight. Not a couple of cheaters after all, just a couple celebrating their anniversary.

And me, off the clock, no infidelity case to investigate. And no need to worry about poor Mélanie Gauthier sitting home alone on Valentine's day while her cheat of a husband pulled a fast one behind her back.

I smiled as I let everything sink in, my fingers finding their way to the locket resting near my heart, the locket I'd inherited from my mom that held photos of my parents as young newlyweds. They were both gone now, but they'd had a happily ever after while they were here, which gave me hope that everyone else could, too. A thought that made me especially glad for the evening's turn of events.

Which got me thinking maybe Laurent was right. Maybe I did believe in fairy tales. Just a little.

## 3

*I* LOOKED INTO the swirling mass of bubbly water. "That's the biggest bathtub I've ever seen," I said. "You could surf in there." An exaggeration, of course. The tub was huge with seating for two and then some. But it was the way the water tossed and turned and created mini waves that got me thinking about surfing. It also had me gripping my stomach hoping my food and champagne would stay put.

Adam came up behind me and circled an arm around my waist. "I know. It's even bigger than it looked in the pictures online. The whole suite looks bigger. This place is awesome. I can see why Camille recommended it."

I could, too. Not just the suite but the whole resort. From the outside, the place looked like a castle and it was nestled on an estate beyond the stuff of fairy tales. In addition to the ski hills, it had a skating rink, a lake, toboggan rides, and horse-drawn carriages. Not to mention an indoor pool, a gym, and spa treatments. And none of that included summer fun around the lake or the boating, horseback riding, biking tours, or golf. A place like this could keep a couple very busy. When they weren't in their suite, they wouldn't have any time for pesky things like talking, which would suit Camille just fine. Probably what she liked best about the place. I, on the other hand, was starting to feel very partial to the king-size bed. It was even more massive than the bathtub and had the distinct advantage of remaining completely still. Not so much as any pea-size lumps, let alone any waves.

"What do you say we relax in the tub?" Adam suggested. "I could scrub your back while we watch a movie."

Slowly, I shifted my gaze to the wall opposite the tub. Sure enough, inset just above a gas fireplace with marble his-and-her pedestal sinks on either side, was a big-screen TV. Clearly, this fairy tale land catered to the dreams of both little girls and little boys.

A knock came from the outer room, and Adam dropped his arm from my waist and strode out of the bathroom. I followed after him and caught up just as he opened the main suite door and a man walked in. Hotel staff, by the looks of him. Starched uniform, shoes shined to glowing, gold ball buttons down his front, wave of thick, black hair slipping out from under his cap as he bent to unload two suitcases and a small nylon duffel bag. He stood and I got a look at his face, olive complexion, hooked nose, pinpoint charcoal eyes, late twenties or a bit older.

He reached in his pocket and pulled out keys and a sheet of hotel stationery. "Your car keys and the information you requested, Monsieur," he said, handing the key and paper to Adam. Both the man's English and his French were spoken with a foreign accent. Eastern European maybe. "If you need anything else, please ask for me, Sergei. I am here all night."

Adam glanced at the paper before stowing it in his own pocket.

He thanked and tipped the valet and the man wished us a happy Valentine's day and left.

"What was that all about?" I said.

"Ah, ah, ah," Adam said, dropping his key ring on a dresser, picking up the suitcases, and depositing them on the luggage stands near the closet. "That's for me to know and you to find out. Later. Much later. And don't even think about peeking in my gym bag." He took off his suit jacket and hung it in the closet, stowing the duffel bag below it and closing the closet door. "I believe there's a warm bath waiting for us."

Right. The bath. With the water tossing about to and fro. Like the buzzing in my head. The buzzing that was urging my eyes to close in sleep, an urge I was determined to ignore. This was the first time in our almost three years together that Adam had gone to so much trouble for Valentine's day. I wasn't about to miss a minute of it.

Adam stepped towards me and slipped to my back, taking hold of my long hair in one hand and hovering his other hand over the zipper that ran up the center of my dress. His warm breath reached my neck a second before his lips. He traced a line of kisses down to the locket skimming my cleavage then over to my shoulder as he slowly unzipped my dress and eased it away from my body, revealing the pale pink bra I'd bought special for the night. The silky feel of rayon tickled as Adam slowly continued to slide the dress down the length of my body past my matching pink panties. He paused, then let the dress fall to the floor where it hit with a thud. A thud much too loud for delicate fabric landing on plank wood flooring. The thud was followed by a louder one.

Adam and I locked eyes and listened as yet another thud sounded, this one traceable to the hallway outside our suite. We ignored it and resumed positions until it went again and Adam groaned, glanced at my lingerie, sighed, and walked off towards the door. I ran to the bathroom, grabbed one of the complimentary robes hanging from a hook on the back of the door and ran back, shimmying up behind Adam as he moved away from the peephole, edged open the suite door, and peered into the hallway.

I stretched my neck to see out around him. At the end of the hall, I zeroed in on the source of the noise. The door to the next suite was ajar and banging against the door frame. Again and again. The tempo uneven, no one in sight. Unlike typical hotel doors, these doors were massive, made of thick solid wood befitting a castle. All rounded at the top with oversized vintage doorknobs and iron keyholes. The banging door included the added bonus of rusty hinges that squeaked with each thud.

"We should close it," I said to Adam. "Maybe they're in the shower and they don't know their door is open. Anyone could just walk in."

"I guess," he said, heading towards the neighboring suite.

I fell in step behind him and heard a new thud. This one sharper. I turned to see our own door had slammed shut.

Adam turned, too, and shook his head. "What are you doing out here? You're not dressed. Get back in the room." He went over to our door and turned the knob. The door didn't budge. He extended a hand to me. "Give me the room key, will you."

"I don't have it," I told him.

He groaned again. "Great. I don't have it, either. Now we'll have to call downstairs from the neighbors' room and get someone to come up and let us back in."

We both went to the banging door and peeked in.

"Hello…" I called out. No answer, so I called again. Still nothing, but I spotted a phone on the credenza nearby. The suite was the mirror image of ours—a sitting area with a kitchenette at one end and wide French doors open to the bedroom at the other side. All in light romantic décor with soft white walls, metal bed, patchwork quilt, area rugs over white plank wood floors. Windows and more French doors leading to a balcony lined the back wall, covered in floor-to-ceiling drapes wrapping around the adjoining wall at the far end. A narrow, stone, double-sided fireplace shared the wall between the sitting area and the bedroom. Unlike the fireplace in our bathroom, this one burned wood and had a few logs crackling away giving off a cozy glow. So the chill in the air surprised me until I spotted an edge of curtain billowing by the balcony doors.

"You call downstairs," I said to Adam, crossing the room. "I'll just close the balcony door. The breeze coming in must have been what made the other door knock back and forth."

Adam tiptoed over to the phone. "We shouldn't be in here without permission."

I shot him a look over my shoulder. "Who we gonna ask? Unless there's someone in the bathroom, nobody's here. And I'm not checking the bathroom. Let's just hurry and get out of here before someone shows up. We can wait in the hall for the valet or whomever to let us back into our room."

"You can't wait in the hall in that robe."

"Sure I can." I turned and flapped my arms at him, extra sleeve dangling from each hand. The robe was one-size-fits all, which in this case meant roomy and tall, not snug and small. My petite body was fully covered and then some, not even any lingerie peeking out. "It's not exactly revealing," I said. "I feel like I've been swaddled by a polar bear."

I continued on my way and pushed the patio door shut. Only it pushed back.

Uh oh. I had no problem being seen in the polar bear robe, but I wasn't keen on being caught in a stranger's room.

I looked back at Adam, phone in hand, quietly humming along to an easy listening tune, probably on hold. To flee or not to flee? That was the question bouncing around in my brain. But even if I ran over and grabbed Adam, we'd never make it out in time.

So I sucked it up and prepared to explain to our fellow hotel guest why we were in the suite uninvited.

Only whoever was outside was taking forever to come in, so I clamped my robe tighter to fend off the cold, opened the door wider, and looked out at the black night. Nobody loitering on the snow-dusted balcony. Nothing in sight but the lighted ski hills nearby, small lanterns twinkling like stars outlining their trails. Their reflection bounced off snow and glinted at me, from on high to down low where my eyes caught another glint. This one caused by shimmer, not lights, that reflected off shiny black shoes, not snow. Shiny black shoes attached to motionless legs splayed flat out on the balcony floor.

**THE LEGS DISAPPEARED** behind a row of three planters shrouded in burlap for the winter, a few dried twigs lodged in the snow below them. Three planters positioned near the wall, making it unlikely that the legs' owner had wandered in between and fallen down.

One of the shiny shoes was lodged at the bottom of the balcony door like a pushy salesman's foot preventing his customer from shutting him out. I bent, instinctively wanting to move the foot to save it from the pain of the door whacking against it. It was a man's foot, I could tell that much because of the shoes and slacks. And I was pretty sure I knew who the foot belonged to.

I took hold of the ankle, gingerly, in case it was hurt, and listened for moaning or other signs of pain. Nothing. The ankle was cold to the touch, even through the black sock, but that was no surprise. At these temperatures, a hot coal would feel like an ice cube in no time. I eased the man's leg out of the door and tried asking if he was all right, but I got no response to that, either. Not a good sign.

I stood and rooted around on the wall for a light switch for the outdoor lamp and flicked it on. Nothing. I glanced at the lamp to the right of the door, a wall mounted gas light replica, no bulb, leaving me in near dark while I tried to assess the situation.

"Adam, get help," I called into the suite behind me. "Someone's hurt. I think it's Sergei. The valet."

With the foot out of the way, I stepped out, tripping slightly on the legs as I tried to get past them so I could squeeze in between the planters to get closer to the body. I sucked in my breath and turned sideways but couldn't get through. I tried leaning over the planters, my robe snagging, my neck straining. I wanted to get a good look at his face, his chest, anything to see if he was still breathing. No go. I couldn't see a thing. I eased out and tugged at the nearest planter, but it wouldn't budge. It was frozen in place along with the other two planters.

I ran back into the suite and made a beeline for the bathroom, passing Adam talking into the phone, shooting me a quizzical look as I whizzed by.

I slowed when I spotted the blow dryer near the sink. I grabbed it and got about two feet before it yanked me back and I saw it was attached to the wall.

"What are you doing?" Adam asked, staring at me from the bathroom doorway.

"I'm looking for something to melt the ice at the bottom of the plants outside," I told him, my eyes darting around the room.

His forehead creased in continued confusion, but he crossed over to the blow dryer. "This thing must come off. Hang on a sec and I'll get it."

It took way more than a sec and I wasn't about to wait longer. I grabbed a glass from the side of the sink, ripped off the sanitary paper wrapper, and filled the cup with hot water. I dashed back to the balcony, spilling drops of water as I ran. I zipped outside and stopped dead, water sloshing out of the glass and plopping onto my feet. The body was gone. Shiny shoes, legs, and all.

# 4

*A*DAM WAS RIGHT behind me, blow dryer in hand, its severed cord dangling. "Where is he?"

I shook my head, words failing me. I looked to the ground for footprints in the snow, scanning for signs of where the guy went, but the earlier layer of snow had been trampled and spread about from all my running around. No discernible prints showed anywhere. Mine or anyone else's.

"You sure someone was here?" Adam asked.

"Of course I'm sure. He was right there." I pointed behind the planters.

Adam stepped closer and peeked around the burlap. "And you sure it was Sergei?"

I shrugged. "I think so. No, I'm sure. He had the same shoes."

There was a tap at the suite door before it opened and a harried looking woman came in, mid-fifties, light hair in a chignon, navy wool suit, jacket unbuttoned, cautious eyes surveying the room.

"Over here," Adam said, ushering me inside and waving to her from where we stood just inside the balcony.

Two men trailed in after her, each wearing hotel duds similar to Sergei's. Both impeccably groomed from their fresh faces to their manicured nails. One sporting a thin gold wedding band on his left hand, the other's hands bare save for a room key. Both early twenties, short haired, and tall, moving like gawky teenagers despite their manly bulk.

The woman looked from me to Adam, introduced herself as Madame Lacroix, the manager, and asked in French which one of us was hurt. Adam explained to her that we were fine then what had happened. Also in French, him being a native Montrealer, his French was much better than mine, albeit with a definite Anglophone accent. Then he switched to English to include me in the conversation and told her that I thought the man on the patio had been Sergei.

After a quick exchange with the Manboys, Madame Lacroix said we had to be mistaken because Sergei had not been on duty since the day before.

Adam and I looked at each other. I had been a bit tipsy. Maybe I got the valet's name wrong. But that wouldn't explain Adam also thinking the guy's name had been Sergei.

We explained about the valet bringing up our bags earlier and depositing them in our room down the hall.

Madame Lacroix wrinkled her nose at us. "This is not your room?" she said, her gaze skimming down to my robe.

One of the Manboys stepped forward and quietly told her we were registered in the suite next door.

"We got locked out," Adam explained. "We were calling down for someone to let us back in."

"Right," I said. "The door to this room was banging and we wanted to help. Then I found Sergei's foot caught in the balcony door." I pointed and everyone looked at the door now shut tight. No foot blocking its closure, no air streaming in and billowing the curtain.

Madame Lacroix walked over to the balcony, opened the door, and looked out. "I see nothing. Everything is fine."

"But he was there just minutes ago," I said. "Just lying there."

She turned to Adam. "And you say the man looked like Sergei?"

"Well, I didn't see him," he said. "But that's what Lora thought."

She looked at me. "You are the only one who saw him?"

I nodded and she glanced at the Manboys who trekked onto the balcony, returning minutes later, shaking their heads, whereupon Madame Lacroix swiveled her head back my way, pinning me with a dubious look.

I returned her look with an earnest one of my own. After all, she may be finding my story hard to believe, but I knew what I saw. "Look, the man may be hurt. Don't you have security cameras in the halls? Maybe you could check the footage. Maybe you can see if he left the room and if he's okay."

She closed the balcony door and studied Adam and me with an expression that intimated she found my suggestion extreme if not ludicrous. Her gaze showed no concern about Sergei but every concern about having troublemaking guests. She continued to eye us as she pulled a phone from her pocket and made a brief call. Almost immediately after she clicked off, her phone buzzed and from what I could understand of her conversation, whomever she was speaking to had no luck locating Sergei in the hotel or by phone. Neither bit of news making me feel any better.

"What's going on here?" someone said from behind us.

We all turned towards the new voice breaking into our conversation. Martin Singleton, standing in the suite doorway. His wife, Mélanie Gauthier, swept up in his arms, her hands linked behind his neck, her head resting on his shoulder, her feet dangling, one shoe balancing on the tip of her toes.

Just my luck. Unless they roamed the halls playing Tarzan and

Jane, this must be their suite. And given Mélanie's bygone days with Camille and Laurent, she'd probably be on the phone filling them in on my escapades before I made it back to my room. If I ever did. The look Madame Lacroix was giving me had me thinking I was one step away from being asked to leave the premises. Probably still swaddled in the white robe, the extra fabric hanging past my hands being used to tie my arms behind my back. And who could blame her? I was in someone else's room claiming to have seen a hurt valet vanish. A valet who wasn't even on duty apparently.

Martin set Mélanie down, advanced into the room, and glanced around, his eyes moving methodically like somebody taking inventory. Then he strode closer to our clique and asked again what was going on, his voice controlled anger, his jaw firming, his eyes starting to flame.

Madame Lacroix went into a speedy explanation in French about the open door and us being locked out of our room and using their phone to call downstairs. Nothing about the valet or about me being crazy. At least not from what I could make out. Whether she believed the story about how Adam and I got into the suite or not, she seemed to be doing a good job of selling her edited version. Martin's face downgraded from angry to annoyed.

Mélanie weaved her way over to stand beside her husband and blinked at me. "You are that American girl? Camille's friend?"

I nodded and smiled.

She trailed her eyes over to Adam. "And this is *ton mari*? The one making the surprise for you?"

"That's Adam," I said to her. "My boyfriend."

"Ah, *c'est ton chum*. Okay." She tottered, grabbing onto Martin's arm for support, and shot Adam a big smile, a smear of lipstick on her otherwise gleaming white, straight teeth. "Stay," she said. "Have some wine with Martin and me. To toast to *Saint-Valentin*. I want to hear everything about your first visit to this *magnifique château*."

I didn't think more wine would do her any good. Or me for that matter. The champagne earlier coupled with Madame Lacroix's stern looks already had me questioning my sighting of Sergei on the balcony. Or even meeting Sergei in the first place.

Madame Lacroix cleared her throat and the Manboys looked at her. She wagged a discrete finger towards the door, her hand barely moving from its place near her hip. The boys lumbered out of the room, and she turned a reserved smile Adam's way. "If everything is settled here, we'll just let you into your room, Monsieur, and everyone can get on with the rest of the night."

Adam started to ask about the disappearing valet, but she cut him off and shot us both warning glares to keep our mouths shut in front of Mélanie and Martin. Hotel 101 peacekeeping I figured, lest we upset their other guests with our unfounded ramblings and they decide to kick up more of a fuss about us letting ourselves into their room uninvited. The latter clearly being the only real issue as far as Madame Lacroix was concerned. And one we could be in real trouble for if she decided to press things, making it plain it was in our best interests not to rile her further.

She nodded "good evenings" at Mélanie and Martin and strode out the door, motioning for us to follow.

"Stay," Mélanie said again, snaring my arm as Adam and I walked by her en route to catch up with Madame Lacroix.

Adam cut his eyes to my arm, his expression idling between amusement and concern. "Let me just grab our room key," he said and slipped out.

Mélanie's lips slid into a sloppy smile and she transferred her grip back to Martin. "Get the wine, *mon cheri*."

Martin patted her hand on his arm, released her grip on him, and steered her over to the armchair in the corner of the room.

When she was fully seated, he went over to the large dresser, a silver tray on top set with goblets and wine sitting beside a large basket filled with fruit, cheese, and chocolate.

"Really, we didn't mean to intrude," Adam said, streaming back into the room. "Maybe we should take a rain check."

Martin turned from the dresser. "That may be best."

"No, they mus, mus, mustn't," Mélanie said, giggling at her own slurred words. "Camille and Laurent would never forgive me. One drink, Martin, *s'il-te-plaît*." She titled her head and batted her glassy eyes at him. The head tilt causing her to lean and slip towards the edge of the chair.

I lunged forward to stop her from falling, and her emerald necklace swayed out and caught me on the cheek. I righted Mélanie and touched my cheek, hoping the sharp stone hadn't cut me.

"You all right?" Adam said, coming up beside me.

I nodded, my cheek starting to ache, my head a bit dizzy. Champagne tipsy didn't bode well with a knock to the face. And I'd been wrong about the emerald. Up close, it seemed heftier and pricier, more than enough to cover the down payment on a car. Probably it could cover the cost of a compact model. At full sticker price.

"*J'm'excuse*," Mélanie said, her voice cracking. She was way beyond tipsy. Flat out drunk was more like it, her emotions so close to the surface her face barely contained them.

"No problem," I assured her. "It didn't even touch me." Liar, liar, pants on fire. "But it's just lovely."

She looked down at her emerald like she just realized it was there. "Martin gave it to me for our *anniversaire*. We got married right here on the day of Valentine. Every year Martin spoils me. Last year, a sapphire, the year before *des diamants*...every time a new surprise." Her glassy gaze flitted away as though she lost her train of thought before she settled back on me. "You too you're having *des surprises* here, no?"

Despite Madame Lacroix's warnings, this seemed like a perfect opportunity to mention the valet on their balcony. It was their room after all. The PI in me really wanted to know if they knew anything about it. "Now that you mention it—" I said, stopping short when Mélanie suddenly slumped forward, head between her legs.

Afraid she might hurl, I grabbed for the tin wastebasket beside the roll-top desk nearby and thrust the can in front of her. Not a moment too soon. A few seconds later, the can was decorated in a sloppy mess of undigested food and booze. All down the sides and pooling at the bottom around a man's shiny black shoe.

---

## 5

*A*DAM SLID THE security latch at the edge of the door into place and turned to face me. "Okay, so there was a shoe in the garbage. It could have been any shoe, right?"

I stood, hands on hips a few feet in front of him. After Mélanie's purging, Martin had ushered us from the room leaving us barely time to say goodbye, and I was left with a healthy dose of curiosity and an unhealthy dose of suspicion. "Sure. Everybody throws away one perfectly good shoe. It's practically a tradition. For good luck, like knocking on wood."

Adam walked over to where my dress still sat on the floor and picked it up. "Look, Lora. I'm just as confused about this thing as you are. But this is supposed to be our Valentine's remember? Don't turn this into some mystery you have to solve. Just 'cause you decided to become a PI doesn't mean you have to find trouble everywhere."

"I'm not. But am I supposed to just forget about seeing a man's body flat out and dead to the world. A body that then ups and disappears? A body that leaves behind one shoe? A body nobody seems to even care about?"

"Maybe," Adam said. "Maybe that's exactly what you're supposed to do. There's probably a good explanation for what happened. Maybe the guy tripped or was drinking on the job and passed out then came around, got up, and left. But even if it's none of those things and something fishy's going on, we've done all we could. If the hotel doesn't want to check it out further, there's nothing more we can do. This isn't some stray cat you spotted on the side of a road. You can't just retrace your steps and make sure he's all right." Adam tossed my dress over the back of a chair and strolled into the bathroom. "I say we forget about the valet, refresh the bath, and pick up where we left off before this mess started."

My stomach lurched. It had settled down quite nicely until Mélanie lost her dinner, then the smell riled me up again. The last thing I wanted was to face churning bath water. Plus, I was torn. I'd worked with Camille and Laurent long enough to know Adam was right. There wasn't much more I could do. I couldn't force the hotel to investigate more and I couldn't call in the police for a possible missing man with cold feet.

I still didn't buy the tripping theory, though. And the man didn't smell like he'd been drinking. I couldn't just forget the whole thing. The social worker side of me wanted to make sure Sergei was all right. And the PI side of me wanted to make sense of what happened.

Then again, Adam *had* gone to a lot of trouble to arrange this Valentine getaway. I didn't want him to think I didn't appreciate that.

"Make you a deal," I said, tiptoeing over to the hotel phone to try one more thing before trying to focus on our evening. "If we lose the jets, I'm with you on the bath."

Adam's grinning head popped into view from the bathroom doorway. "Deal," he said. "Give me five minutes, then come in."

"Sure," I agreed, my hand veering off from the phone to our complimentary food basket. With Adam watching, I didn't want him to guess what I was really doing so I bent over the basket like I was considering my options, scrounging past the fruit in search of chocolate. No luck, just fruit. No chocolate, no cheese. I plucked a strawberry and popped it in my mouth, thinking maybe you had to be frequent guests like Mélanie and Martin to score the chocolate and cheese.

When Adam's head cleared from view, I grabbed the phone and called downstairs asking for Sergei. If the guy really was fine and had left on his own, he had to show up sometime, right? Adam and I couldn't both have imagined Sergei doing his valet thing in our room earlier. He had to be around here somewhere. Yet I was told again he was not available and offered assistance from my new phone buddy, Tony, who I was assured in broken English would be more than happy to help me with anything I desired. Which was so not true because what I desired was to see Sergei, up and around, shoes firmly planted on his feet, ankles warm and toasty.

I declined Tony's offer of help and disconnected.

"Ready," Adam's voice called to me from the bathroom.

I cradled the phone, Adam's car key next to it catching my attention. The key Sergei had passed Adam less than two hours earlier when he'd wished us a happy Valentine's day and told us he would be on duty all night. As I headed into the bathroom to join Adam, I wondered what had changed Sergei's on-duty status to off. And I hoped his new status wasn't permanent.

"WHAT ARE YOU DOING?"

I looked across the room to Adam, in bed, shirtless, the quilt dropping to his waist as he sat up. The contours of his shoulders defined by the soft light sifting in from the sconces I'd left on dimmer in the bathroom.

"Nothing," I said.

He checked his mobile set on the nightstand. "It's after one in the morning. Have you slept at all?"

I backed away from the peephole in the suite door that I'd been manning off and on for a while. "Of course I've slept."

Completely true. I'd fallen asleep in Adam's arms and slept for a whole blissful half hour until I heard the hum of the elevator and gotten up to see who was putting it to use in the middle of the night. Nobody I could see, since the doors were already sliding closed and the hallway was clear by the time I reached the peephole. But maybe somebody had gotten on. Somebody who'd been hiding Sergei's body and was now spiriting it away under dark of night.

Adam looked at me, disbelief plain on his face.

"Well, I got a little sleep," I confessed. Just not any after I talked myself into believing the dark-of-night-body-snatching thing. Maybe it was because I'd started the night in work mode or maybe it was something else, but my mind kept turning back to Sergei. Seeing his body lying outside, unmoving and cold, had put a serious wrinkle in my Valentine mood. Not to mention my image of this place as a fairy tale castle. Fairy tales were not supposed to have disappearing bodies.

Adam patted my side of the bed, empty except for rumpled bed linens and the wrapper from the mint I'd found on my pillow. "You'd probably have better luck at sleeping lying down than standing up," he said. "You're not a horse."

I glanced at the bed and back at the door, considering things.

"Seriously, you've got to let this go, Lora," Adam said. "Ever since you started training to be a PI, you see crime everywhere. I'm sure the guy just tripped or something, maybe even banged his head and was dazed for a bit, then got up and left. All on his own. No mystery. No nothing."

I nodded. Sure, that was possible. Although I still thought tripping behind planters wedged close to a wall was a bit of a stretch. "Maybe. But how does that explain Sergei bringing up our bags when everyone says he wasn't working?"

Adam scratched his hair then rubbed some sleep from his eyes. "I don't know. Schedule mix-up probably."

"What about Madame Lacroix not being able to reach him?"

"So he didn't answer his phone. Big deal. If everyone who didn't pick up a call was considered missing, half the world would be reported."

"And what about the shoe in the garbage?"

"We don't even know whose shoe that was," Adam said. "Heck, we don't even know for sure if it was Sergei out on the balcony."

Some logical points. But that was expected. Adam was a digital game designer. He dealt in logic all day. I, on the other hand, dealt in instinct. In my experience, logic always lagged behind instinct. Instinct was like an express bus—it took the direct route to a conclusion. Logic was a city bus, making oodles of stops along the way to round up facts and taking its sweet time getting to the end of the line. A gal could wait forever for logic to make its way to a conclusion. Especially if logic got bogged down in traffic.

I wasn't about to let Adam's logic bog me down. Half the time, nobody believed Nancy Drew when she was onto something, either. And she was always right. She was an instinct girl like me. And my instincts were telling me something bad had happened to Sergei. I couldn't just ignore that. He may need help. Plus, there was a part of me that wanted to prove to Madame Lacroix that I was right about Sergei. I didn't much like her looking at me like I was just some fruitcake, heavy on the bananas. I knew I shouldn't care what other people thought of me. Especially a stranger I'd probably never see again. But I did care. I cared a lot.

Another sound came from the hallway and I looked out the peephole again. Some guy pacing the hall with a baby in a stroller. Probably using the motion to lull the baby to sleep.

"What?" Adam asked, his voice nearly in my ear as he sidled up next to me, his body now cloaked in the twin version of my hotel robe. "Someone out there?"

That was another drawback about logic. Even in firm believers, it was easily trumped by curiosity.

Adam tied the sash on his robe, edged me over, and looked through the peephole, dipping back a few seconds later, disappointment on his face. "Is there any aspirin in this place?" he said as he massaged his temple. "This whole thing is giving me a headache."

More likely it was the bottle of champagne he'd polished off while we were in the bath that was giving him the headache. Neither of us drank often, but unlike me, Adam could sock away alcohol like water, never feeling a thing until it socked him back much later.

"I don't know," I said. "I'll check if there's a medicine cabinet." I ambled into the bathroom and searched the only cabinet in the space, a tall number in the corner behind the tub. Plenty of extra towels, terry cloth slippers, matching tub pillows, a set of loofas, bottle of bath salts. Even a set of snazzy rubber duckies. But no aspirin or other medical supplies. "Nothing in here," I called out.

When I got back to the main room, Adam had already shed the robe and burrowed himself back into bed. I thought about offering to call the front desk to ask my new buddy Tony to send up some aspirin, but the rumble of a snore stopped me. Adam wasn't big on snoring, the snore was probably also compliments of the champagne. Probably he was conked out this time and wouldn't wake up until checkout time. I crawled into bed beside him, closed my eyes, and tried to take Adam's advice and get some rest. There wasn't much else I could do until morning anyway. And the snoring was starting to give me my own headache.

**THE NEXT TIME** I opened my eyes, it was after two A.M. and a low whirring squeak grated in my ears. The squeak came from the corridor, and I was up like a shot, eye to the peephole in time to see one of the Manboys from earlier rolling a luggage trolley by my door. The trolley had only a few bags on the bottom and what looked like dry cleaning hanging from the top. Manboy stopped at a suite across the way, unloaded two of the suitcases, set them aside, and stood a moment at the door. Half a minute later, he reloaded the suitcases and rolled his trolley farther down the hall, stopping at what I guessed to be Mélanie and Martin's door, my peephole not having the range to see that far.

I put my ear to the crack at the side of my door and listened, hearing what I thought was the click of a door opening. I eased my own door open to get a look and spotted the trolley down the hall but no Manboy.

Odd time to be dropping off luggage. Not a lot of guests checked in or out at this hour. Or so I thought, until Martin stepped into the hall. He was fully clothed in the same suit as the night before and he had a navy overcoat slung over his arm. I pulled my head back so he wouldn't see me, leaving my door open enough to listen for Mélanie but I didn't hear her.

The squeak started up again and I heard Manboy and Martin talking in quiet tones headed this way. I rushed to close my door before they got close enough to see me. Watching through the peephole, I saw them get into the elevator, trolley and all.

I dipped back, thinking it was odd for Martin to be leaving in the middle of the night. Seemed to me there were a lot of odd goings on in the suite next door. Which did nothing to quell my concerns for Sergei. I peeked out through the peephole again at the empty hallway. Hmm. Probably a quick look-see couldn't hurt. I threw on the polar bear robe over the blue satin nightie Adam had brought for me, eased on my pumps, slid my room key and phone into the robe pocket, and slipped out. I crept over to Martin and Mélanie's suite and put my ear to the door. I heard nothing but quiet on the other side, so I moved closer to listen harder and was rewarded with a loud snap. Only it came from below me, not from inside the suite.

I looked down at my shoes, one had grown brown scraggly wings, nearly thin enough to blend in with the dizzying carpet design. I lifted my foot and saw the two scraggly wings came from a broken twig, surrounded by more twigs littering the base of the doorway. Twigs just like the ones around the planters on Mélanie and Martin's balcony. Twigs I was sure weren't in the hall earlier when Adam and I had left. I bent to get a closer look, and a whoosh of cool air blew out at me, followed by a stiff hand that grabbed my arm, yanked, and pulled me up and into the cold air.

# 6

---

*I* HEARD A door close behind me as I scrambled forward, trying not to trip on the mountains of extra robe swinging around my legs.

"You have to help me," Mélanie said to me as she let go of my arm. Her French accent made the "Hs" silent in her words, her voice was breathy with panic. She stood two feet in front of me, dark eyeliner smudged, ginger hair tangled down the back of her black negligée, short shrubbery branch in her left hand. She started pacing, puffs of black fake fur and feathers falling from her heeled slippers. "He knows, he knows. I'm sure he knows." She paused in her pacing and her negligée puffed around her from a wind gust coming in from the balcony door, open again.

"Who knows what?" I asked, inching over to close the balcony door, peeking outside briefly before shutting it, relieved to find the porch clear of bodies this time.

She waved the shrubbery at me and began pacing again. "Martin. He knows about me and Sergei. I am sure."

Her and Sergei. Woah, was she talking an affair? Laurent told me Mélanie and Martin were perfectly happy. Nobody was supposed to be cheating. That was so not Valentine friendly. Although it might explain how Sergei ended up on the balcony, shiny shoed toes to the air.

"You and Sergei what?" I asked, secretly hoping they were long lost siblings or something but bracing myself for the worst.

She stopped and stared at me like I was asking the color of the sky. "Sergei works here at the hotel," she explained as though it was new information to me. "We were married. He was my husband before Martin. You are friend of Camille and Laurent, no? Then of course you know."

She made those last two statements like the one foregone conclusion inevitably led to the other. Like Camille and Laurent talked about her all the time. And like they were in the habit of revealing personal details of their friends' lives. Which they weren't. They were French and freer with self expression than most people I knew, sure. Adept at self protection, absolutely. But they were also fierce about the protection of friends and family. It was one of the things I valued about them. Apparently, Mélanie never picked up on it.

"No, I didn't know," I told her. And it seemed I wasn't the only one. Seemed Martin had been in the dark about her previous marital status, too. But an old husband didn't sound so bad. Certainly better than a current lover. At least I felt better about it. And I didn't see it as a cause for the events of the evening. Or for her sudden need of my help. There had to be more to it.

Mélanie pointed the stick towards the closet, one door slid half ajar. "He's gone. I woke up and his coat was gone. He knows and he's left me. On our *anniversaire*." She paused, her voice breaking as though she was about to cry. Then the stick went flying through the air and I automatically ducked, watching as the branch whizzed past me and pierced a pillow on the bed. The tip of the stick disappeared into the pillow, the rest of the branch stuck straight out like an arrow. A quivering arrow, not a nice sturdy Cupid arrow.

"*Salaud!*" she said. "How could he do this to me?" She turned and looked directly at me, her eyes moist and wild. "You've got to bring him back."

"Me? You want me to go after him?"

She bobbed her head up and down in a nod, one that was jammed on instant replay. "You are investigator with Laurent and Camille, no? Finding people is what you do."

Not entirely but that wasn't the point. "He'll probably come back on his own," I said to calm her, hoping she didn't have another branch handy as I moved closer, noticing the slight tremor in her body, the sweat breaking out on her upper lip. My old social work training kicked in and I pulled the throw blanket off the end of the bed and wrapped it around her shoulders. I rubbed the sides of her arms as I walked her over to the armchair near the desk and lowered her down to sit. I kept up the arm stroking until her tremors downgraded to shivers, her adrenaline easing off some. I stepped back and watched her as I spoke again. "Look, I don't know what happened between you and Martin, but it will blow over. These things always do." Not that I had a clue if this was true. Sergei's inert body on the balcony might signal otherwise in this case.

Mélanie shifted in the chair and crossed her legs, dangling one furry slipper in the air as her free leg rocked back and forth. "You have to find Martin. He does not understand. I have to explain to him."

"Sure," I said. "In the morning, I'll go out and see if I can find him." Maybe. If Martin was gone, he was probably on his way back to the city by now. And if foul play was afoot and Martin was responsible, then finding him would be a job for the police. Sergei was who I was worried about at the moment. But Mélanie had no way of knowing I'd ever met Sergei, let alone seen him flat on his back on her balcony.

Or maybe she did. Maybe she knew exactly what I'd seen. I had no idea, but I needed to find out what she did know without leading the witness. I decided to use my social worker technique of asking an open ended question rather than hitting her with one too direct or that she could easily brush off with a one-word response. "If you want my help I need to know more," I said. "What exactly happened with Martin and Sergei?"

She sprang up, nearly knocking me over. "There's no time for talk. The morning is too late," she said. "We need to find Martin now." She went over to the credenza, grabbed her purse, thrust her hand inside, and pulled out an iPhone, slim model, gold flower skin on the back. She punched in a number and held the phone to her ear, speaking into it an instant later. "C'est encore moi, mon amour. Je t'attends," she said then tapped the screen and set the phone beside her purse.

Her urgency and fevered tone were upping my own anxiety. "Look, Mélanie, you better tell me what's going on."

"I told you. We need to find Martin."

"Right. You said that. But why is it so important we find him fast?" I gravitated towards the balcony again. "And where's Sergei?"

Her face darkened, her eyes skimmed over to the pillow with the branch sticking out of it. Her gaze moved on to fix on the suite door. I looked over too, a fumbling noise in the hall catching my attention.

Mélanie ran for me and marched me to the balcony door. "Martin," she hissed at me. "He's back. Hide. What will he think to find you here in the middle of the night?" She pushed me out onto the balcony.

"It's freezing," I said, already feeling the chill air biting at my cheeks. "I can't stay outside dressed like this."

She waved a hand at me. "Only for a few minutes." She closed the door before I could protest again.

I tried the knob, but it wouldn't turn. Jammed from the cold or locked, I couldn't tell. The woman had to be crazy leaving me out here in the dead of a winter night, me wearing nothing but a nightie and a robe. A polar bear robe, maybe. But only in size, not insulation.

I danced from one foot to the other, my shoes even less insulated than my robe, and I knocked on the door but nobody answered. I bobbed around the glass in the door and tried to find a gap in the curtains so I could see inside. The only view I managed to get showed a sliver of the room with no sign of Mélanie or Martin. Just an eyeful of the bed, rumpled sheets free and clear, headboard piled high with pillows, plump and covered in white cotton lace. One pillow still impaled by the branch. Perfectly centered. A bulls eye worthy of a pro archer. Or maybe a crazy woman bent on hiding secrets from her husband. A woman in the habit of ridding herself of pesky problems by shoving them onto the balcony. And leaving them to freeze to death.

# 7

---

*I* GOT OUT my cell phone and called Adam, but he had his mobile going direct to voice mail. I disconnected and called Camille who also had her calls going straight to message. So I left her one telling her that her friend was having a meltdown and had locked me on the porch. Then I pulled up my browser to find the hotel number and call downstairs to get them to send someone up to let me in, stopping myself mid search when it occurred to me that may not be such a hot idea. How would it look to find me on the balcony desperately trying to get into a room that wasn't mine? I'd already been found in the suite once under dubious circumstances and come dangerously close to being escorted from the premises. Possibly in a loony wagon. With Mélanie nowhere in sight to vouch for me, this time I could be looking at a paddy wagon.

So I ditched the call to the front desk and tried the last contact I wanted to be calling in the dead of night: Laurent. I so did not want him to know I'd gotten myself locked outside, seven stories above at twenty degrees below. It had taken some convincing to get him to let me train as a PI for his agency, and the last thing I needed was for him to question my ability to take care of myself and change his mind. Only I needed not to freeze to death more and that trumped my dread of calling him.

He picked up after the first ring, his voice deepened by sleep but alert. "Trouble in paradise, *mon petit lapin?*"

"You might say that," I said through chattering teeth. "Your old girlfriend Mélanie locked me out on her balcony. I can't get back in."

"Mélanie was not *ma blonde*, only a girl on my street."

Really? Correcting me about his dating history took priority over taking in the fact that I was locked outside on a cold winter's night? I wanted to roll my eyes but was afraid they'd freeze in perpetual worship position. "Forget that. Looks like she's gone off and left me here, and I need you to call her and get her to come back and let me in. Fast."

"I take care of it," he said, his accent deeper from sleep, too. "Keep your phone close."

The call cut out and I walked around some to keep my circulation going, alternately rubbing at my arms, passing the phone from hand to hand, wondering if this same thing had happened to Sergei. Maybe he'd been stuck on the porch like me, nobody around, nobody to hear his cries for help what with all the windows locked up tight for winter.

I glanced at the row of planters, dimly illuminated by the light streaming out through the thin curtains on the French doors. Maybe Sergei had wedged himself in behind the planters to escape the wind and cold. An idea I would seriously contemplate myself if I wasn't so creeped out by the subsequent loss of consciousness and possible death that befell the planter's previous lodger.

My eyes scanned for another way out of the cold and landed on the nearest balcony. Mine and Adam's. Not attached. And at least ten feet away. No help there. I shimmied over to a window over-looking Mélanie and Martin's porch. I dropped the phone into my pocket and flexed my fingers, already numb and rigid, until I got enough mobility to try the window. Locked. I went back to the door and knocked again. Nothing.

I rooted around in the snow some, looking for clues about what happened to Sergei, trying to distract myself from the feeling of blood slowly freezing in my veins. That got old fast and I gave up and squatted down to conserve whatever heat I could, wrap-ping the extra robe fabric around two layers thick as far as it would go and sinking my head down into the collar. My ears ached and my teeth clacked so hard I could barely think. Probably not more than five minutes had passed but it felt like forever. I'd be a human popsicle soon. If Martin had wanted to spoil Mélanie with jewelry, he was way off the mark with an emerald necklace. That woman needed a watch. If she had intended to let me back in quickly as she promised, that is. And that was a big IF. Growing bigger by the minute.

As was my impatience and what I was sure was frostbite nipping at my nose. I stood and wrenched the burlap cover off one of the plants, wrapped the rough fabric around my hand and fore-arm, turned back to the door, and launched a punch at the glass pane near the doorknob, clinching my eyes closed at the last second to protect them from flying shards.

"*Heille là*, That's some way to greet *ton sauveteur*."

I opened my eyes to see Laurent standing in front of me, hand patting his stomach. His naked stomach, taut and bare and framed at the sides by the dress shirt he had on earlier, now hanging loose and open over jeans, buttoned but unbelted.

I dropped the burlap to the floor and massaged my knuckles, glancing at the now open door, its glass still intact. "Did I just?—"

He nodded and tapped a pink splotch of skin on his stomach.

"*Oui*, Lora, you did." He scanned the balcony, pulled me inside, and closed the door. "Now tell me, my PI coming in from the cold, what kind of trouble you are in this time?"

**MY EYES NARROWED** and some heat streamed back into my body. "This trouble has nothing to do with me," I said. "And what are you doing here? How did you get in? I thought you were tracking down Mélanie."

"You were freezing outside. I was two floors away. It was faster to come myself." He didn't bother to explain how he got into the suite. Which was fine by me. Laurent wasn't big on law bending. Probably he'd talked some poor maid into letting him in.

I blinked at him. "Two floors away? You didn't tell me you were staying here." I tilted some to peer around him and lowered my voice. "Are you, um, with someone?" It was Valentine's after all. Given the trail of women Laurent always had drooling after him, I couldn't imagine him ever spending a Valentine's alone.

He cocked an eyebrow at me. "Are you? When I left the *souper*, you were with your Anglophone. He is not here anymore to help you?"

"Of course he's here. He's sleeping in our room and his phone is off."

"He's in your room and you are here? Alone? Ah, *oui*, I understand." He tried to keep his face serious but a grin crept onto his lips.

Geez. Even in the middle of the night, the guy couldn't give teasing me a rest. "You understand nothing," I said and went on to tell Laurent about the body on the balcony, shiny-shoed toes to the wind, and Sergei's now-you-see-him-now-you-don't act and Martin's clandestine departure in the wee hours of the morning and Mélanie's prowess with branch throwing. I finished up by pointing over to the branch, heretofore to be known as exhibit A, and did a double-take when I saw that it was gone. I walked over, climbed onto the king-size bed, and made my way up the middle to the pillows piled at the top. "It was here. I swear. Stuck in one of these pillows."

I hunched on all fours, moving the pillows around in search of the object of Mélanie's target practice. I shuffled the pillows carefully at first, then quickly when I couldn't find the right one. No pillow with a branch. And no pillow with a small hole in the center of its pillowcase. I heard an "Oomph" from behind me and turned my head to see Laurent had caught a pillow in the face. Probably I should have toned down my shuffling.

"*Vraiment*, Lora," he said. "Is this new violent streak of yours something we should talk about?" He had major bedhead going on, his feet were as bare as the skin between the gaps of his open shirt, and his scruff accentuated the intense look he directed at me.

"Sorry." I sat back on my haunches and sighed. "I didn't mean to bean you with that. But it's crazy. The pillow was still here when I was out on the balcony. Where could it have gone?" My eyes scanned over to the chair by the desk, but it was empty as well. Then I noticed the closet, the sliding doors moved from where they'd been open before to now reveal the other side. Mélanie's side. Empty too. And her purse was gone from the bureau. I jumped off the bed and ran to the bathroom. All clear. Nothing left but damp towels and a ring around the bathtub.

I whizzed around to zip back out to the main room, and I slammed into Laurent's hard body instead. An eyeful of skin came at me and my nose grazed a patch of dark chest hair, taking in the lingering smell of zesty soap mixed with sleep sweat.

Laurent reached out and steadied my shoulders. "Easy there. Running on wet floors is not good. You could break one of your lovely legs."

I looked at the floor and saw a trail of water on the tile, small droplets from the bathtub to the tall cabinet in the corner. I picked my way over, careful to avoid the drops, and yanked open the cabinet door. As bare inside as Mother Hubbard's cupboard. Not so much as a complimentary bottle of shampoo in sight. Just four crooked, vacant shelves, the bottom one damp with water.

"See? Now do you believe me?" I said. "That's not normal. Mine and Adam's cupboard has no water in the bottom. It has extra towels and bathtub toys and stuff."

Laurent tilted his head in my direction. "Bathtub toys? We are both adults, Lora. You don't need to use *un euphémisme* with me."

"I'm not using a euphemism. I'm talking bath salts and scrubbies. Get your mind out of the gutter. I'm telling you a man's gone missing and is possibly hurt or dead, and your old friends are acting fishy. Focus, will you. And button your shirt while you're at it."

He grinned at me as he started to do up his shirt. "You get bossy when you miss your sleep, eh. Violent and bossy. I will remember that."

I frowned. Bossy and violent. That wasn't the image I wanted my boss to have of me. And it wasn't how I felt. If anything, I felt confused and frustrated. Some exhaustion spiked with residual adrenaline thrown into the mix. Probably that accounted for my mood. That and the fact that I was still in thaw mode from my frosty furlough on the balcony.

"Look," I said, thinking maybe I needed some time alone to regroup. "I'm good now. I'll figure this out. You can go back to your room. I'm sure your date is wondering where you are."

"*C'est la deuxième fois,*" Laurent said so low I could barely hear him.

I stepped back from the cupboard to hear better. "Excuse me?"

"That's the second time you asked about my love life." He

slipped in front of me, crouched down, and peered into the base of the cupboard. Then he shifted, stood, and followed more water droplets on the floor toward the bathtub where he bent over the drain, pulled his phone from his pocket, and took a picture.

I moved in beside him and tried to see what he thought worthy of documenting, my view partially blocked by his body. "So? You ask about my love life all the time. Anyway, I'm only trying to be polite. I feel bad about interrupting your Valentine's night. When I asked you for help, I expected you to make a phone call not a house call."

"The prince never makes phone calls in a fairy tale. The prince rides in and saves the princess."

I righted myself and crossed my arms over my chest. "I supposed you're the prince in this scenario? I've got news for you, Prince, this princess didn't need saving. I could have broken in from the balcony any time I wanted, as you'll recall I was in the process of doing when you got here. But I was trying to avoid roughing up the place. I'm in enough trouble with the hotel staff already. They didn't believe word one about what I told them about Sergei. Nobody believes me."

"*C'est pas vrai*. I believe you. And if you're right, your missing valet may have left more than his shoe behind when he disappeared into the night."

Laurent stood, allowing me a better view of the drain. And the gold bulbous button nestled in the bottom.

I glanced at the button. It looked exactly like the one I'd seen on Sergei's jacket. I leaned over the tub, trying to get a closer look to be sure, my hand automatically coming up to keep my locket from dangling too far forward as I bent. Only my hand met with air. No locket. I straightened and felt my neck. Empty. No chain, no locket, just skin. Skin quickly gathering heat, my accelerating pulse fueling the blood in my veins like a forest fire, spreading steadily, smoldering under my flesh. It was gone. My mother's locket. It couldn't be.

I tried to remember the last time I'd felt the locket and a sudden flash hit me of when I was dipping between the planters outside, trying to get to Sergei. I held the image in my brain and ran for the balcony, desperately hoping my mother's locket hadn't disappeared into the night along with the valet.

# 8

---

"**A**RE YOU SURE you didn't take it off?" Laurent asked me. He stood a few feet away from me near the desk in the suite. His eyes still glazed from watching me root around outside, mining every inch of snow like a frenzied gold digger.

I flailed my arms at him and bits of twig flew off me and drifted to the floor. "Of course I'm sure! I never take it off when I'm away from home."

He stepped closer. "Okay, okay. *Calme-toi, mon lapin,* it has to be here somewhere. We'll find it. Maybe you should check your room again."

After my mining on the balcony came up empty, I'd ran back to my suite and searched every place I'd been, paying close attention to the bathroom and the bathtub. My hunt was fast but thorough, no help from Adam who was still so conked out he'd only groaned and covered his face with a pillow when I'd swamped the suite with light for my search and rolled him over as I frisked the bed. The locket was nowhere to be found.

"It's a waste of time." I worked to hold in a sniffle. "It's gone. My mother's locket. Just gone. And on Valentine's day of all days. This is supposed to be the day of love and happily ever afters. This is so not happy." My lip trembled at the corner of my mouth. My British ancestry had blessed me with a stiff upper lip that was threatening to loosen like a broken dam. That loosening could lead to blubbering and all sorts of emotions could leak out and turn into a full-blown flood in no time. I couldn't let that happen. I had to have dropped my locket on Sergei, and I needed to focus if I wanted to find him and get my locket back. I had no time for an emotional flood.

I willed my mouth to tighten and mumbled through clenched lips, "Maybe we should call the police."

Laurent cast a gentle smile my way as he picked a twig out of my hair. "I know how important it is to you, but I don't think the police will help with a lost locket."

"Not for the locket," I said, wandering over to the kitchenette. "For Sergei." I opened drawers until I came across a box of baggies, withdrew one, inverted it, and headed off to the bathroom. I cloaked my hand in the baggie, went over to the tub, and retrieved the button from the drain. I stood and removed my bag glove, peeling it off so it turned right-side out again with the button safely enclosed. If I'd learned one thing from Laurent and Camille since joining their PI firm, it was to treat possible evidence with care.

I held the bagged button up to Laurent who had come in behind me. "I'm thinking we show this button to the police and tell them about Sergei's disappearance."

He took the baggie from me. "I don't think it will help."

"How can you say that? I told you I saw buttons like that on Sergei's jacket." As an ex-cop, Laurent was big on following proce- dures, and I figured notifying police in circumstances of mysterious disappearances like this was usual protocol. Surely he had to agree.

He shook his head. "You saw buttons like this on a valet jacket. In a hotel with many valets. We don't know for sure the button is Sergei's or what it means if it is. It's not enough. We need more. Some proof."

I held in a groan of frustration. This was the "shoe in the garbage" conversation I'd had earlier with Adam all over again. Men and their incessant need for logical proof!

I stopped myself from telling Laurent about my instinct versus logic theory. On several PI cases, we'd gone rounds on my instincts being downgraded to hunches while his and Camille's were elevated to educated guesses. I didn't need to hear the lecture again. I'd hoped my hunches had graduated by the end of a previous case but maybe not. Thing is, this wasn't just about finding Sergei anymore, this was about finding my locket. And holding in my flood of emotions over my mother's lost locket just may have redirected them to my defensive channel. "I thought you said you believed me," I huffed out.

Laurent looked down at me, holding his eyes on mine. "I believe you saw a man on the *terrasse* outside. Probably even Sergei. But what happened to him after that," he paused to shrug his shoulders, "nobody knows."

"Somebody knows," I said. "Call Mélanie. She has to know something. Sergei was on *her* balcony, and she was married to the guy and seemed very nervous about Martin finding out. This can't all just be a coincidence. Plus, the woman asked me for help then ditched me on the balcony. That's just odd."

"It will do no good to call now. It's the middle of the night."

"Exactly. It's been hours since Sergei disappeared. We're losing time. Try her." I caught a reluctant look on Laurent's face, so I added a "please" and tried to soften my eyes into a sweet, persuasive gaze. Not an easy move at this hour. Probably coming off more Daffy Duck than demure damsel.

He closed his eyes briefly, took in a breath and released it slowly before pulling out his phone and making a call. A beat later, he disconnected and dialed again. "No answer at house or cell."

"Well try Martin. Someone has to know something."

"I don't have his cell number," Laurent said, stowing his phone in his pocket. "No point in calling his work at this hour."

This was getting us nowhere. And it was exhausting. If only Madame Lacroix would have looked at the security footage. Then maybe I'd have some proof to satisfy Laurent. I went to sit on the edge of the bathtub, and Laurent's hand wrapped around my upper arm, holding me in place, keeping me from making contact with the tub.

I glanced at his hand, or maybe glared was more like it. I wasn't so sure about Laurent's description of my lack of sleep state turning me bossy and violent, but a tad grouchy was probably a fair bet.

He held tight, meeting my glare with cop face—the one accessory he hadn't turned in along with his uniform when he'd left the force. "Crime scene," he said.

I let my eyes roll upwards and down again. "Make up your mind already. Is it or isn't it?"

"*Ben*. Until we know it's not, we treat it like it is."

"Look, the place is full of my cooties already. It's got to be at least three in the morning by now. I need to sit."

His grasp held fast, his eyes darkened, and his gaze moved past me. I followed it to the big screen TV mounted on the wall between the sinks, just like the one in Adam's and my suite.

Seriously. Men's endless fascination with mega inches of plasma baffled me.

"Geez, it's a TV. Not the Mona Lisa," I said. "And it's not even turned on."

Laurent released his grip on my arm and pulled me to him. "Shush."

I stopped talking and the sound of hushed voices came to my ears. Voices coming from the other room, not the TV. My heart rate kicked up a notch. I so did not want to be caught in the suite uninvited again. I automatically assessed the bathroom for hiding places and came up with zero. No shower, no curtains, no hampers. Nothing. Just the giant bathtub, standing free and exposed. And the tall cupboard in the corner, still damp and harboring its wobbly shelves, which even cleared out would only have enough space to hide one of us.

I dashed for the only available shield, the open bathroom door, and slipped in behind it, Laurent's hand at my back, hurrying me along. He slid in after me, and grafted his body onto mine, pinning us both against the wall, his other hand grabbing the door knob and tugging the door towards us, so near it almost bumped my nose.

"Don't move," he murmured into my ear.

Fat chance of that. He had me packed in tighter than a turtle hiding in its shell. A warm shell, pulsating to the tune of Laurent's heartbeat, echoing my own.

Footsteps drew closer, two sets, both holding back their full weight. Laurent's grip on me tightened, his breathing growing shallow and matching mine, breath for breath.

The door shook and my breath caged itself in my chest, throwing off our duet.

"*Mais voyons, vous deux,*" a female voice said. "You got me out of bed for a game of *cache-cache?*"

At the sound of the voice, my breath flew from its cage and I craned my neck to see past Laurent. A woman in a wrinkled silver dress, stiletto-heeled silver pointy shoes, and blonde tousled pixie hair looked back at me. Camille. Standing about six feet tall in the heels, her brows furrowed, her hands waving about in the air.

Laurent released his grip on the knob and we filed out from behind the bathroom door.

The two siblings bantered back and forth in French, their words sprinting out like they were neck and neck, nearing a finish line. I caught only the odd word of what they said—something about a valet on the *terrasse* in a housecoat. Which made no sense, but I didn't care. My attention focused on the man coming up behind Camille. The dark-haired man in the dark suit and dark shoes sporting dark rings under his eyes. And carrying a pillow in one hand and a branch in the other.

**I RUSHED FORWARD.** "YOU FOUND THEM," I said, reaching the guy holding the pillow and branch. It was Puddles, Camille's current bedmate and Valentine's date.

He looked down at me then averted his eyes. "I don't want to know what you two were doing before we got here. If Adam asks, I was never here." He thrust the pillow at me and walked out of the bathroom.

Camille glanced from me to her brother and narrowed her eyes at him.

"What are you talking about?" I asked, stepping out after Puddles, shifting the pillow under my arm. "And what are you guys doing here?"

"You left me a message about Mélanie locking you outside, no?" Camille said, coming up behind me, inserting herself between me and Laurent. "You don't think I'm going to come?"

"I didn't think you'd get my voicemail until tomorrow. You came all the way from the city that fast?"

"*Non, non.* We were here. My phone was off for a while only."

Geez. Was everybody here? The place was fab, but there had to be other Valentine's getaways. Briefly, I wondered how they got into Mélanie and Martin's room without a key, but since Camille was more flexible on the law-bending thing, sometimes it was best not to know some things so I didn't ask.

She folded her arms across her chest and tapped one foot on the floor. "*Dis-moi*, what's this Laurent tells me about a valet taking your locket? Give me his name. I'd like to remind the man about the ten commandments."

I smiled despite my panic over the lost locket. Camille was a Catholic by birth, but I suspected her reminder would have less to do with the ten commandments and more to do with her ten belts in martial arts. "The valet didn't take it," I told her. "I think I dropped it on him and he may have absconded with it accidentally. He's gone missing. Didn't Laurent explain that bit to you? And he wasn't just some valet. It's Sergei, Mélanie's ex-husband. One minute he was on the balcony, flat on his back, still and quiet as a stone, and the next minute, poof, gone."

Camille strode over to the patio door and switched on the defunct outdoor light, muttering under her breath when it failed, pulling out her phone. She went outside, holding her phone aloft, panning it back & forth, then came back in, her eyebrows furrowed. "Looks like Sergei didn't disappear on his own. *Le terrasse* is a mess. Looks like two raccoons went at it out there."

Laurent grinned and I pretended not to notice.

"Um, that was me actually," I told her. "I was looking for my locket."

Her brow furrow reversed direction. "*Alors?*"

THE LOST LOVE LIAISON

I shook my head. "No, nothing. I couldn't find it. It's gone. We need to find Sergei and see if he's got it. And to make sure he's all right, of course."

She turned her attention to Laurent and motioned him over to the kitchenette for a sidebar chat. Their conversation took on their usual French speed-talk and I turned my full attention to Puddles and shook the pillow at him. "Where did you find this?"

He pointed the branch towards the bed. "Under there."

Under? I hadn't looked under the bed. It was kitted out in romantic, cozy layers of bedlinens that included a bed skirt. I'd thought there'd be a platform below like lots of other hotel beds. Hugging the pillow to me, I crossed to the bed and crouched down to take a peek underneath. All clear. Nothing more stashed underneath except a few dust bunnies. And if they'd witnessed any suspicious activity, they weren't giving up any secrets.

But at least now I had exhibit A. With both Sergei and the branch disappearing, it had been tough to prove I'd seen anything. Even the gold button find wasn't much help. The reappearance of the branch and pillow were at least proof I'd seen something, right?

I shifted the pillow back to my arm, relieved Puddles of the branch, and brought it over to Laurent who had gone curiously silent, his back to the kitchenette, his focus on me. "Here," I said to him. "This proves I was right. It's your friend Mélanie with the violent streak, not me. She could have taken someone's eye out throwing this thing around."

In the mirror over the desk by Laurent, I caught sight of Camille and Puddles exchanging a look. Then I saw my reflection, pillow tucked under one arm, the other arm up, brandishing the branch at Laurent as though I was about to call out *"en guard."*

Laurent smiled and eased the branch from my grasp. "You

don't have to convince me Mélanie has a temper. The whole neighborhood knew that. She slashed the tires of every boy at *l'école secondaire* who broke her heart."

Hmm. A tire slasher and a human popsicle maker. Not an appealing résumé. Especially in a woman who couldn't hold her booze.

"Those boys deserved to have their tires slashed," Camille said. "They had no interest in Mélanie. Only her father."

Her father. Ew. "Please tell me there's more to that story," I said.

Camille gravitated over to the bureau across the room and peered in the abandoned gift basket. "*En fait,* not really. The father of Mélanie was a singer long ago when he was young. A local celebrity in Québec. Nobody you would know, but to date his daughter was a big deal. Something the boys could brag about to their friends."

"Oh," I said. "That's crummy." And not a good start to dating life for anyone. I'm not sure I agreed with Camille that it called for tire slashing, but then Camille had a different take on justice than I did. Mine involved righting wrongs and a strong belief in karma. Hers involved lashing tongues and a strong dose of kickass. "But then Mélanie married Sergei," I added. "So he must have been different from the others. He must have had real feelings for her."

Camille shrugged. "Sergei she met at *l'université.* A foreign student here for one semester only. She married him so he could stay in the country. But she'd seen too many American movies. It doesn't work like that here. *Le mariage* does not guarantee citizenship."

That last bit wasn't news to me. As an American who had applied to the Canadian government for dual citizenship, I knew something about the immigration laws. Things were easier for me because my mom had been Canadian so I had a right to apply based on that, but I'd learned the process wasn't so easy for everyone and marriage was not a given loophole to the laws.

"But Mélanie and Sergei probably still loved each other," I said, joining Camille over by the bureau. "After all, she did try to help him. That's got to mean something, right?"

Camille let out a long breath. "Not everything is about love, Lora. Not everyone is a *romantique* like you."

Puddles raised an eyebrow on those last points, but Camille didn't seem to notice. Camille considered herself lacking in the romantic gene. I suspected the gene wasn't missing, just dormant for the time being, waiting patiently for Camille to realize being committed to a relationship was not on par with being committed to a nut house.

Her eyes trailed over to the gift basket again. "Sergei was a cause for Mélanie. *C'est tout.* She married him on an impulse and divorced him just as fast when her father told her she was breaking the law and could be arrested and go to jail."

I glanced at Laurent. "You could have mentioned some of this before."

"I didn't know," he said. "I had a nice car with good tires. I stayed clear of Mélanie."

"Could she really have been arrested?" I asked.

Camille shrugged. "She could have been in some trouble I guess. The *gouvernement* doesn't like it when people abuse the system. The family has kept the circumstances of *le mariage* a secret ever since just in case."

Oh boy. No wonder Mélanie was so worried about her past coming out. Somehow Sergei must have found another way to stay in the country when the marriage fell through, though, or he wouldn't still be here. I wondered if Mélanie had helped him figure something else out or if he'd managed that on his own.

"So how do you know so much about it?" I asked Camille.

"A mutual friend was a witness at Mélanie's first wedding."

Ah. A mutual friend with a greater affinity for disclosure than discretion it seems. Maybe that's why Mélanie never told Martin about Sergei. With disloyal friends like that, not to mention the gaggle of boys dating her for bragging rights only, it wouldn't surprise me a bit if Mélanie had some trust issues and had learned to guard her heart. The question is, was her heart and fear of the law all she was guarding against or was there some other reason she hadn't told Martin of her previous marriage.

"I'm guessing this friend never blabbed to any stoolpigeon types or there'd be no reason to still keep the whole thing private," I said. "But I'm seeing a pattern here. Mélanie doesn't seem so great at choosing the people in her life. How much do we know about Martin? Is there a reason she'd think she couldn't confide in him about everything? I mean, the guy is her husband. They have two kids together. You'd think she'd trust him by now. At least enough not to rat her out for some long ago mistake."

Camille glanced at me, her smeared eyeliner underscoring the questioning look she threw my way. "*Ben*, you mean would Martin go after Sergei like a passionate, jealous fool?"

"Something like that."

Camille fingered a chocolate in the basket, her face pensive. "Martin is a pencil pusher at some company downtown. He's too boring to have the *passion* to murder anyone."

Yikes. Camille's brain was going straight to murder. Not what I wanted to hear. I was still holding onto hope that we'd find Sergei sooner or later, safe and sound. Along with my locket. "I don't know about murder," I said. "But something happened to Sergei. A man doesn't just lose consciousness wedged behind tubs of plants and then up and disappear all by himself. And Mélanie did seem pretty thrown by her secret coming out. She thought Martin had left her because of it. And now they're both gone, too. That makes no sense. What are the chances they'd leave their anniversary getaway in the middle of the night?"

"Pfft. So they had a fight and ran off," Camille said. "*C'est normal*. Everybody does that."

I sighed. More Camille logic. She bolted from the slightest sign of trouble with a man faster than the lead horse in a stampede. "And you think it's also normal to leave someone out on a balcony to freeze to death?" I asked her.

She waved her hand in the air, part dismissal part surrender. "*Voyons*, Lora. It doesn't matter. Your locket, that matters. That we get back. Give me an hour and I'll find your missing valet," she assured me and stuck her hand back in the gift basket and pulled out a brightly-colored ball of foil-covered chocolate.

"*Laisse ça*, Camille," Laurent said, dropping the branch on the bed and coming up behind me. "Don't touch anything."

She paused, her fingers nearly done unwrapping the sweet smelling ball. "*C'est du chocolat*, Laurent. *Ce n'est pas une preuve de crime*."

"Camille," he said, warning in his voice.

"Laurent," she said back, mocking in her voice. She popped the chocolate in her mouth before Laurent could protest again and headed for the door.

Puddles glanced over my head to Laurent then to me, shook his head, and went out behind Camille, nabbing a banana from the basket on his way out.

I turned to Laurent. "You think they'll find Sergei?" I asked him.

"You know Camille. What she'll find is some chump to get her into the hotel computer system. And into their employee records. Then probably she'll find her way to Sergei's house. If he's there, problem solved."

"And if he's not?"

Laurent scanned the room, his dark eyes hard to read, fatigue cloaking them with something more than cop eyes. "Then we might not be leaving by checkout time."

I looked down at the floor and steadied my voice. "And if Sergei doesn't have my locket?"

Laurent moved closer and settled a warm hand on the back of my neck. "Then we're definitely not leaving by checkout time."

## 9

---

*A*DAM WAS STILL snoring away in bed when I crept back into our suite. I tiptoed past him to the bathroom and considered Laurent's suggestion that we both get a little sleep and let Camille take over the search for a bit. Sounded smart and reasonable. Unfortunately, my emotions were feeling anything but smart and reasonable. Now that I had a moment alone, my stiff upper lip trembled and my eyes squeezed tears onto my cheeks as I caught a glimpse of myself in the bathroom mirror, sans locket, the dimmed sconce lights throwing shadows across my chest where the locket should have been.

My mother's locket meant everything to me. It held her energy and her love. It was my connection to her, to both my parents really. As long as I had it, I felt like they were still with me in some way. And now it was missing. No way was I getting any sleep.

I allowed myself a few more tears, dried my eyes, rinsed my face, and told myself to buck up. Sergei couldn't stay gone for long and when he surfaced, chances were good the locket would, too. Surely with all its motherly love tucked in it, the locket would have to find its way back to me. It was Valentine's after all. The day for love miracles, right?

Problem was, a miracle could take a while. And every minute the locket was gone was a minute too long. Another minute for it to get farther away. I didn't have time to wait for a miracle.

Quietly, I went over to the closet, pulled out the overnight bag Adam had brought for me, and took out some underwear and the only outfit he'd packed me: Jeans, a white tank shirt, and a cowl neck sweater I'd never seen before, something blue and fluffy that looked like it needed a good brushing. A gift maybe. Not my usual look but I appreciated the thought. And the warmth, once I got it on along with the other clothes.

"Adam," I whispered going over to the bed. Nothing. Not a peep. So I tried again, louder, and got a moan, immediately followed by a sputtering snore. I gave up trying to wake him out of his champagne coma, and I went to the desk to write him a note bringing him up to speed on things and letting him know I was going out to search the hotel for my locket. Or Sergei. Whichever I found first.

I slipped the note under the edge of the table lamp, jumping when I heard a thud behind me. I turned. Nothing out of place and no one anywhere in sight.

Geez, the hotel may be like a castle straight out of a fairy tale, but I could seriously do without all the bumps-in-the-night business.

My eyes scanned over to Adam, still sleeping peacefully, arms hugging a pillow to his side, slight occasional snore. The champagne-sedating effects aside, he'd always been a sound sleeper and now I thought I knew why. He traveled a lot for work and had probably grown used to the occasional racket of hotels. It was a skill, really. A kind of traveler's selective hearing. The same way parents learn to tune out their kids' frequent ruckus, only zoning in on true signs of trouble.

Probably if I was a parent or a traveler I'd have that skill, too. But I wasn't, so when the thump went again, I tracked it, getting as far as the bank of windows at the back of our room before it stopped. My heart skipped a beat, thinking someone was outside on our balcony. Some guy in a parka, pistol in one hand, pot of hot coffee to keep him warm in the other. Just waiting until the right time to bust in and attack innocent guests in their sleep.

Not that I really believed that. Not really. That was just my imagination working overtime from lack of sleep and the stress of the night. I was almost sure of it.

I gathered my courage, bolstered by the thought that surely Adam would wake up if I should need to belt out a blood-curdling scream, and I reached for the knob on the balcony door, pausing when the thump went again. Coming from somewhere to the side of me, not to the front, not from the balcony.

I pivoted, switching direction, and crept closer, shuffling the curtains, feeling my way, the dim light of the bathroom sconces not shedding any light in this corner of the room. The noise went again, louder now, when I got to the last panel of drapes. I shoved the curtains aside and a sliver of light by the floor caught my attention. The kind of light that streams in from under a door. A door heretofore completely hidden by the floor-to-ceiling drapes that curved out beyond the window wall and wrapped around to cover several feet of the adjoining wall. A wall I now realized housed a connecting door between our suite and the one next door. Mélanie and Martin's. The suite we'd all vacated barely ten minutes earlier and left dark.

· · ·

**FROM BELOW THE** CRACK, the sound of another thump drifted out, clear and sharp now with whispered voices following the noise. I knelt and put my ear close to the strip of light, straining to hear more, wondering if Mélanie and Martin had returned. Or maybe Camille and Puddles.

A patch of darkness appeared in the strip of light, and on reflex I pulled back, raising my head and shifting to crouch mode. When the dark shadow passed, I leaned in again to listen, this time resting my ear flat to the door, placing my hands against the wood on either side, allowing it to support some of my weight as I balanced on the balls of my feet. Something shifted at my fingertips, my feet rocked, and the door gave way, sending me sprawling forward, spilling onto the floor, my mouth taking in a mouthful of curtain.

I spit out the fabric, finding myself on my hands and knees on the other side of the connecting door, tangled in Mélanie & Martin's drapes. I wrestled myself free and scooted backwards in retreat, hoping nobody had spotted me conspicuously shrouded near the wall, invading their privacy like a lunatic fan.

I made it to the threshold then halted in my bare-toed tracks when the voices cut out, along with the lights. The last thing catching my eye before everything went dark, a man's black shiny shoe nestled in a wad of curtain gathered on the floor.

**I STAYED COMPLETELY** motionless on the border between the two suites, sure I'd heard a door close but unsure if anyone was still lurking in the dark. I couldn't hear any sounds of movement, just the distant sound of Adam's snoring. I inched towards where I'd seen the shoe, my brief glimpse of it in the light showed no signs of Mélanie's partially digested Valentine dinner, but the shoe was definitely familiar. My guess was Sergei's other shoe. I was also guessing I'd just found the answer to how he made it off the balcony and out of sight so fast while Adam and I were wrangling the blow dryer in the bathroom. He must have passed through the connecting door. Either alone or possibly with the aid of whoever may have helped him onto the balcony in the first place.

My money was on the second scenario. If Sergei had simply accidentally fallen then recovered and left as Adam had suggested, it seemed more likely he would have gone out by the main suite door. And *not* sans shoes.

Which is just what I planned to tell Camille and Laurent when I called them to tell them about my finds. Just as soon as I had the shoe for added proof, that is.

I felt around in the dark, tapping my hand over pooling curtain on Martin and Mélanie's side of the border, pausing when I made contact with the shoe. Covering my hand with the edge of my sleeve, I lifted the shoe towards me but it yanked back. Stuck. On something I couldn't see. Something on Mélanie and Martin's side of the door. Something I'd have to get closer to if I wanted to release the shoe.

Listening carefully, I moved to the curtain on Mélanie & Martin's side, found the slit in the fabric between panels, and peered out, one-eye style, into the suite. Faint light glowed out from the closet on the far wall, and in the dim light the room looked undisturbed from what I could tell. No Mélanie or Martin. No Camille or Puddles. No big goons.

Which got me wondering if maybe Camille was right and Martin and Mélanie had just checked out and gone home, and what I'd heard was housekeeping coming in to make sure their guests unusually early clear out hadn't included the TV.

With that in mind, I glanced behind me, then eased myself through the curtains and slowly tiptoed through the main room to the bathroom to make sure I was alone. No hotel staff or fellow guests or big goons in there, either.

I set the lights on dimmer like I had in my bathroom, crossed back to the connecting door, and bent to check what had caught the shoe's laces, finding them snagged on an old door jamb. I freed them and was about to pick up the shoe when I remembered the plastic bags in the kitchenette, so I fetched one first then used it to pick up the shoe like I had done earlier with the button in the bathtub.

The shoe didn't quite fit, but I figured it was a bag-half-full kind of thing, tucked the bag under my arm, and crept back to the bathroom to shut the lights, anxious to leave now that my mission was accomplished. Midway back, the opening bars of Pink's "Get the Party Started" rang out, and I flinched then froze, darting a look around the room for unwanted company. Seeing no one, I checked the nightstand for a clock radio, finding it bare except for a Tiffany lamp knockoff and vintage style phone.

The music played on so I followed it, letting my ears guide me, inching closer as I traced it to behind the bureau where flashes of light radiated out along with the tune, illuminating the wall in bursts. The unmistakable blinking of a cell phone. I bent down and fished it out. A phone with a gold flower skin on the back. Mélanie's. Caller ID lit up the screen with "SAM" then faded away as the caller rang off, something else catching my attention behind the bureau before the light disappeared. Something long and shiny.

I sucked in a breath and broke out in a wide smile. Long and shiny like a necklace chain. My locket!

I held the cell in one hand and reached in again with the other to get the necklace. My smile dimmed and my heart sank when it came into full view. Not my locket after all. Just Mélanie's Valentine emerald hanging from its gleaming chain. Probably it and her phone had fallen and been left behind in her hurried rush to leave. I stood and fisted the necklace. Frustrated, disappointed, and most of all annoyed with myself for getting my hopes up.

"I'll take that," someone said from behind me.

I jumped at the voice. A man with an accent I couldn't immediately place. A man with a mean case of garlic breath hitting me sideline in the face as he grabbed me from the back, ensnaring my body with a vice grip that squeezed the air out of me, my lungs expelling the air in a grunt.

## 10

*I* FELT THE shoe drop out from under my arm and the phone slip from my hand. The man squeezed me harder, the room blurred and came into focus again. A surge of fear clamped my stomach, and I felt the early stages of panic rising to my head, adding to the dizziness already setting in from my lungs being squeezed.

*"Oh no you don't," I silently told the panic. "You're not going to send me over the edge. If I'm going to pass out in a man's arms on Valentine's Day, it is not going to be the arms of this garlic breather."*

I wanted to scream but his grip on me was too constricting, so I expressed myself with hand signals, punching out at him with my fisted hand and trying to loosen his hold on me with the other. He held tight, so tight I couldn't even weave my fingers in between us to get a firm grasp on his arm, let alone do any pulling. I heard him laugh at my attempt, and instant anger replaced the fear in my belly. Anger that made me stomp my heel on his foot and bite his arm. He cursed and bent into me, and I used the opportunity to take advantage of our height difference and bang the back of my head into his throat. He gurgled and released his hold on me, not fully but enough for me to wiggle out and run away from him to the closest door, the main entry to the suite, yelling for Adam as I ran, hoping to goodness he wasn't still too conked out to hear me.

I flipped the lock and yanked the knob, but the door wouldn't open. I tried again, yanking harder, surprised when the handle wouldn't move. Someone had to be holding it from the other side. I stretched onto my toes and looked out the peephole, but all I saw was a blur of light with flecks of tarnished green here and there, like looking into the reverse end of a dirty telescope.

Garlic Breath grabbed me from behind again, his hands grubby and rough, this time pinning my arms behind my back and shoving a wad of fabric in my mouth, something big that held my jaw open, something that tasted suspiciously like balled up old sock.

Lights blinked on, and I craned my neck at the sound of Adam's voice, seeing him standing blurry eyed and unsteady, hotel robe open over his boxers, gazing at me from just inside the connecting door. He stepped towards me and Garlic Breath flung me around, using me as a shield, then he torpedoed ahead and hurled me into Adam, knocking both of us back a few feet and onto the floor.

Adam hit the ground first, breaking my fall, his head smashing into the metal bed post on his way down, his eyes closing, his body growing still when it reached the wood floor. I landed sideways, barely hitting the ground before Garlic Breath came at me again, hovering above, reaching for my clenched hand.

The necklace. He wanted the necklace. It was the only thing I still held, both the shoe and Mélanie's mobile having dropped when he grabbed me.

Glancing up, I got a look at Garlic Breath's face and recognized him as one of the Manboys from Madame Lacroix's entourage. And he wasn't alone anymore. The other Manboy was coming up behind him, gawking down at me then shifting his gaze to Adam, whose inert body barely made contact with my back, the pulse of his breathing beating a steady drum on my spine.

"What are you doing?" Manboy2 said, his eyes on Adam, his voice ending in a squeak.

"What do you think I'm doing," Garlic Breath wheezed out over me. "I'm trying to get the damn emerald. Is it my fault she won't stop squirming around?"

"But the man," Manboy2 said. "He's not moving."

"He's fine," Garlic Breath huffed. "Just help me before the guy wakes up."

I flailed at him, praying he was right and Adam wasn't badly hurt, and I wrenched the sock from my mouth, screaming for help. With one hand protecting the necklace, I had only one hand left to mount a defense so when Garlic Breath got close enough, I called in my leg troops and kneed him in the chest, hard, aiming for the soft spot in the center. He grunted and slowed, giving me time to get in another knee-hit, this time aiming lower for an even softer spot. He froze and moaned, still hovering over me, then shoved Manboy2 towards me, leaving me only a split second to roll away and take refuge under the bed with the dust bunnies, hoping with all my might that the Manboys would continue to ignore Adam and focus on me since I had what they wanted.

I scrambled to the head of the bed, towards the center, nestling the necklace and pulling myself into a ball, as far out of reach as I could get. Trying to buy time while I sorted out what was happening or until help arrived. I wasn't so sure giving the Manboys the necklace would just make them go away, but I didn't think I could stave them off for long. Plus, I was worried about Adam. I knew he was breathing, but he was also unconscious and that's never good. He could have a concussion and I needed to get him help pronto.

A big arm swooped in at me, fingers grazing my legs. Then midway up the bed's underside Manboy2's face appeared, bent and shrouded in bed skirt.

He frowned at me and swatted his arm out again, closer this time. I pushed myself away, wedging my body in the corner, and I yelled for help as loud as I could, wondering what was taking so long for somebody to hear me. All the nearby guests couldn't have traveler's hearing, could they?

*"Ta gueule!"* I heard Garlic Breath snap at me from somewhere above, telling me to shut up, as Manboy2 shimmied partway under the bed, his hand clasping my ankle and giving it a strong yank.

I kicked at his head with my other foot, calling for help again, wishing I had my mobile. Or Mélanie's. He lost his grip on my leg, and I scurried out from the bed and knocked straight into Garlic Breath, headbutting him in the shins. He stumbled back, crashed into a standing lamp, and fell over. I winced, both at the pain in my head and at watching him land with a crack, back first, on the iron carving jutting out of the lamp base, and lay still.

Behind me I heard a grunt and as I stood, I turned to see Adam and Manboy2 in a scuttle on the other side of the bed. They were moving so fast it was hard to tell who was winning, but at least Adam was up and around. I grabbed the hotel phone extension on the nightstand and glanced over at Garlic Breath, motionless and whimpering, his body still cresting the lamp. I looped the necklace over my head and punched numbers into the phone, trying to reach the front desk, my fingers shaking and having a hard time connecting with the buttons.

Adam called out my name and I turned back to the scuttle, my mind shorting when I caught sight of both men on the floor, Manboy2 sitting on Adam's back and grinding his face into the carpet. I jumped on the bed and tried to whack Manboy2 on the head with the phone, but it wouldn't reach. Damn hotels and their short cords.

I kept an eye on the fight and tugged the phone cord, hard, until it snapped free from the wall. I raised the phone above me, its vintage heft making me totter some on the cushy mattress, then I lunged at Manboy2, trying to take aim as he squirmed with Adam. I saw an open shot and thrust the phone at Manboy2 just as Adam's fist landed on Manboy2's cheek, spinning his head, and the phone caught him across the back of his neck. He swayed, let out an "oof" and a "grock," and slumped to the ground.

Adam and I exchanged a look.

"Omigod," I said. "He's not dead, is he?"

## 11

*A*DAM SKIMMED HIS eyes to Manboy2. "I don't think so. I think he's still breathing." Adam moved to step away and his foot tangled in something hanging out of Manboy2's pocket. He pulled his foot free and tossed the thing aside, and I did a double take when I saw an emerald gleaming up at me. I grabbed for the necklace circling my neck. Still there. That meant there were two emerald necklaces. Same setting, same size, same chain.

Manboy2's hand straggled out and stuffed the necklace back in his pocket, his head turning as he stared my way, blood dripping from his nose onto the white floor.

The suite door flung open and my eyes shifted to the newcomer. Mélanie, blinking wildly and darting a look around the room, her eyes stopping when they landed on me, towering over the bed, her emerald necklace around my neck.

Behind her, Camille, Puddles, and Laurent rushed in, displacing Mélanie, each nearly bumping into the other as they came to a halt. Seconds later, a few strangers appeared in various states of dress, neighbouring guests I figured. Finally roused from their sleep.

Laurent moved first, securing the room. Moving Manboy2 to the chair over by the desk and assessing Garlic Breath still on the floor by the lamp. Camille took action next, tossing her phone to Puddles with instructions to stand by to call for medical help if needed as she cleared the room of onlookers.

While the onlookers filed out, Madame Lacroix strode in and scanned the room, lips pinched, tiny lines notching her mouth like grooves in a plum pit.

Garlic Breath raised himself from the floor and limped towards her, pointing at me and barking out words in French in a tone that seriously challenged its heritage as a romantic language.

When he was done, Madame Lacroix closed the distance to me. "That is your necklace?" she said, gesturing to the emerald weighing down my chest.

I slipped off the bed and planted my feet on terra firma. "No," I said. "It belongs to her." I gestured at Mélanie then pointed to Garlic Breath. "And that valet or whatever of yours was trying to steal it." I slid my pointed finger over to Manboy2. "And that one was in on it, too."

She eyed me. "*Très intéressant.* They just told me the same thing about you," she said. "And you are the one who is not supposed to be in this room. But here you are again, in a room that is not yours."

"That's ridiculous," Adam said, rubbing the back of his head, coming to stand beside me. "Lora is not a thief. She was trying to protect the necklace from those two."

"You are not helping, Monsieur," Madame Lacroix said to Adam, then she turned to Garlic Breath and instructed him to call the police.

Garlic Breath shot me a smug smile as he pulled out his phone, something dropping from his pocket. Something he quickly bent to pick up, stopping when his back froze, half bent, midway to the floor. No doubt still sore from his tango with the iron lamp. He yelped, bringing a hand to his back.

At the sound of the yelp, all eyes in the room moved to him. All eyes except Laurent's which caught mine as he hurried forward and scooped up the object that had fallen from Garlic Breath's pocket.

Laurent cupped the object in his palm and said something I couldn't hear as he showed his find to Madame Lacroix, whose face contorted like she'd accidentally eaten a moldy piece of cheese.

Mélanie came to life from over by the bureau where she'd been rooted since she arrived. She stepped over to us. *"Tout ça* because of Martin's present for me? *Vraiment?"* She reached out to me and made a pinching motion with her hand like a toddler beckoning for his bottle.

I lifted the necklace off my neck and handed it to Mélanie. "There's another one," I told her. "Exactly the same." I pointed to Manboy2. "In his pocket. I'm not sure which one is yours."

Everyone looked over at Manboy2 who shifted in his chair, silent, dabbing the back of his hand at the few remaining drips of blood slipping from his nose.

*"Bouge pas,"* Camille said to him as she went and leaned over him.

He shot her what appeared to be an attempt at a death ray look and she shot one back, hers promising more pain than simple death. She patted his front pockets, slipped her hand in one, pulled out the duplicate necklace, and pinned him with an even darker look.

Madame Lacroix sucked in a breath when the necklace was in plain view.

"It's not what it looks like, Madame," Manboy2 said to her.

Seriously? He was going to deny it. The guy wasn't even a good liar. His voice cracked when he spoke and his eyes kept shifting, their orbs darting back and forth so fast it was hard to make out the color. Grey maybe, with spots of green. Spots of green that looked vaguely familiar.

I went to the door and looked out the peephole. Same blurry view as earlier, only this time no color, just clear blur. I opened the door and looked through the peephole from the hall side, waving my hand in front of the peephole on the inside. A perfect view.

I closed the door and looked at Manboy2, thick sweat now on his upper lip and more forming on his forehead.

*"Qu'est-ce qu'il y à?" Camille asked.*

"The peephole," I said. "It's reversed."

Puddles brushed past me and checked the peephole. "Sure," he said. "Makes sense. You want to know what I think? I think those two valets are nothing but two-bit thieves. Plain and simple. I think they rigged peepholes into people's rooms. I think they watch and wait until guests are out and their valuables are in and then they steal them without anyone the wiser. Classic scam for the not so classic crook."

Puddles had lived an underground life for many years while he was sorting out some messes in his life, and he had run into enough folks in hiding who were underground for less favorable reasons, so he learned a thing or two about scams.

"Think whatever you want," Garlic Breath said. "You can't prove nothing."

Laurent rounded up both emerald necklaces from Camille and Mélanie, took them over to a lamp, and studied them, looking up when the room filled with   "Get the Party Started" again, coming from under the bureau this time, light flashing out in beat with the song. Mélanie's phone. It must have skittered under after I dropped it. Or maybe been kicked under when everyone came rushing in.

I stepped over, fished out the phone, and passed it to Mélanie, noticing the same "SAM" caller ID appear in big letters across her screen. My eyes skimmed over to the bagged shoe I'd also noticed sitting to the side of the bureau. That, too, must have been kicked away at some point and I'd forgotten all about it. I'd even forgotten about Sergei with all the goings on since Garlic Breath grabbed me. I picked up the bag and turned to see Martin had arrived and was peering over his wife's shoulder at her phone.

"Sam?" Martin was saying. "Who's Sam?"

I was curious about that, too. But the look on Mélanie's face told me I probably already knew the answer.

# 12

TEN MINUTES LATER, he was back. Sergei, sporting the same suit he'd worn when I met him, minus one button and plus several creases. His look rounded off by socked feet, a huge bruise above his left eye, and a fresh scab along his eyebrow.

Mélanie had been encouraged to return her call from SAM— Sergei's name reduced to initials—and he now stood in the kitchenette telling his story to one of the cops who arrived mere minutes before him.

Another cop was questioning Garlic Breath and Manboy2. And I bet it wouldn't be long before the cop had enough information to ferry both valets off to the local police station, the PDQ.

Since I already knew most of their story, I listened for only a bit before tuning in on Sergei's while he explained that he owed his black eye to Garlic Breath when a fight broke out after Sergei discovered Garlic Breath spying on his ex-wife Mélanie through the peephole peepshow and going through her things. Sergie's cut eyebrow was courtesy of the planter he'd fallen on during the fight, which made its way to the balcony, where he'd been left by Garlic Breath who'd heard someone coming and hightailed it out of there. But Sergei was then found by Mélanie while Adam and I were wrestling with the blow dryer in the bathroom. Mélanie thought Martin had discovered her secret marriage and was responsible for Sergei's injuries. She hustled Sergei away to keep him safe, fearing it was Martin in the bathroom and he'd come back any minute.

I learned a few more things as I pieced together snippets I'd overheard from both conversations. Like that the Manboys had lied when they said Sergei was not on duty. Probably they fudged the schedule in the database, too. They had no idea where he'd gotten to, but they wanted to keep him quiet about the peephole peepshow and were anxious to find him before anyone else. And they could do that better if nobody else was looking.

"So where have you been all this time?" I asked Sergei.

He turned a sheepish smile my way. "In a tiny room downstairs. Mélanie wanted me to stay there until she and Martin left. She worried for me."

"But didn't you tell her that it wasn't Martin who hurt you?"

"For sure," Sergei said. "But she didn't believe me. She said I didn't have to protect her from the truth. But it was her who protect me." His smile grew more shy. "I thought maybe she still had the care for me. And I do what she wanted. I would do anything for my Mélanie."

I slid a look at Mélanie. She, too, had put herself out and already admitted to a small freak out when she thought I'd seen Sergei's shoe in her garbage. Then again when she found herself with blood on her clothes from Sergei's cut and his button in her pocket. In her second freak out, she cleaned up and tossed out everything in the bathroom, afraid something she touched would have lingering traces of blood.

As she listened to Sergei now, her face was pink, her eyes fixed on the wall. Beside her, Martin was sullen while he tried to explain away the two emerald necklaces to a third cop. Whatever story he was telling, I didn't think the cop was buying. I could read the incredulity on the cop's face from clear across the room. Clearly the cop wasn't as seasoned as Laurent who'd perfected his blank cop face so expertly it reminded me of the guards at Buckingham palace.

I could see that face now as he made his way over to me and dropped something in my hand, something warm from his own hand and so familiar my heart contracted, recognizing it before my eyes registered it. My locket!

"Where did you find it?" I blurted out louder than I intended.

In a lowered voice, he told me it was what had fallen from Garlic Breath's pocket earlier. The thing he was trying to reclaim when his back seized.

Adam moved in to my side. "You didn't tell me your locket was gone, Lora. When did that happen?"

"While you were sleeping," I told him. "I was looking for it everywhere."

Adam glanced over my head to Laurent. "That's the second time today you helped us out," he said, placing his arm across the back of my shoulders and hugging me to him as he spoke over me. "Thanks again. You're a good friend."

Laurent grinned at Adam. "*Ben oui*," he said, his accent especially thick, his French more broken than usual. "Always happy to be friendly with Lora."

Adam's arm on me stiffened, but I barely noticed. Just like I barely noticed the cops rounding almost everyone up and whisking them off the to local PDQ for more formal questioning and probably some booking.

Me, I was too happy to pay much attention to any of it. Sergei was fine and I had my locket back. All was right with the world.

# 13

---

"**Y**OU READY?" **ADAM** asked me.

I scanned the suite, making sure I hadn't left anything behind. "Yup."

"You sure you're not forgetting anything?"

"I don't think so."

He held his hand out to me, gift bag dangling from his fingers. A shimmery white gift bag with burgundy tissue paper sticking out the top.

I accepted the bag, big smile on my face. "Oh Adam. It's too much. You already gave me this trip." My eyes skimmed over to the breakfast tray on the bed, chocolate croissant crumbs on the plate, bowl of chocolate dipped fruit practically licked dry. Glasses of champagne orange juice drained.

He stepped back and snapped a picture of me with the new camera I'd given him as his Valentine's present. The camera he'd been eyeing for weeks. "Open it," he said.

Gently, I lifted the tissue paper out and peered into the bag. Empty except for a stamped envelope that I pulled out to find my name and address printed on the front. The return address covered with a blank blue stickie note. I looked up at Adam, intrigued, as he passed me a letter opener that I used to shimmy open the letter seal.

My smile grew back the minute I saw what was inside. Even by the top edge of the paper I knew what it was. I could make out the government letterhead. My Canadian citizenship papers! It was official, I was now a dual citizen of the good old USA, my birth-place, and of Canada, the birthplace of my mom.

Instantly, my fingers sprang to my locket and tears sprang to my eyes. I'd been waiting months for my papers to come. They were going to change everything. Now I could stay in the country indefinitely and take on permanent full-time work as a PI at C&C as soon as I finished my training.

"This is the best Valentine's ever," I said to Adam.

Adam laughed and touched the bruise on his chin, thankfully that and a slight bump on his head his only souvenirs from his scuttle with Manboy2. "Only you would say that after spending the night worrying about a disappearing valet, freezing on a terrace, getting attacked by peeping tom thugs, and being accused of theft. And let's not forget losing your mom's locket."

Losing my locket wasn't exactly accurate. According to a text I got earlier from Camille, when Madame Lacroix asked Garlic Breath to check the balcony vis-à-vis the validity of my claims about the disappearing valet, Garlic Breath had seen the locket and pocketed it.

"Yes, but everything worked out in the end," I reminded Adam. "That's what counts."

At least everything worked out for me. Mélanie Gauthier still had to deal with a cheating husband of sorts, who, also according to the text from Camille, had admitted that one emerald necklace was real, the other fake. And after giving Mélanie the real necklace, he'd planned to switch it out for the copy. Leaving her with the cheap one and him with the expensive one. Something he did every year on their anniversary. Bought her extravagant jewelry, had it insured, photographed, and then replaced with a copy so he could return the original and keep the refund for himself. A plan he devised a few years into his pencil pusher job at an insurance company that paid him little in salary but well in cheat scheme ideas.

But this time he had a witness. Garlic Breath who'd been watching through his peephole peepshow and seen Martin futzing with the two necklaces, recognized the scam, and saw an opportunity to cheat a cheater by switching the necklaces back, taking the real one and leaving Martin with only the copy. And no recourse for Martin to report the theft without outing himself.

And Garlic Breath's plan would have worked, too, if Mélanie hadn't accidently dropped the real necklace behind the bureau, making first Martin lose track of it and dip out in the middle of the night to see if he'd dropped it somewhere, and then leaving Garlic Breath unable to find the necklace when he went to the room to steal it. Not a good surprise for either of them.

And not one for Mélanie, either, to come back to retrieve the phone and necklace she'd left behind only to find a room full of people and two necklaces. Definitely not her best Valentine's I'd bet.

"It's nearly checkout time," Adam said. "We better go."

I nodded and tucked my citizenship papers in my purse.

Adam grabbed our overnight bags and headed for the door. I followed him out, nearly tripping on the nightie trailing behind him.

"Hey," I said. "You're dropping my stuff. My bag's not closed right."

He set the bags down, bent, and shoved my nightie back in. "You got too much stuff. It doesn't all fit."

"It's the same stuff you packed to come and it fit then." I looked over his shoulder into the bag. "Wait. That's not mine. How did that get in there?" I pulled out the plastic baggie with Sergei's shiny shoe. The one I'd picked up after I fished out Mélanie's mobile the second time. I must have brought it back to our room after all the hubbub died down.

"I don't know," Adam said. "I just threw everything in after breakfast when you were in the bath."

We both turned when we heard a door thud down the hall. Mélanie. Coming out of her room. Alone. Looking sober and subdued. Finding out your husband has been using you to stash some extra cash on the side can do that to a woman.

The elevator tinged, the doors opened, and Sergei walked out, darting a look at Mélanie then blushing when he caught sight of me and Adam.

Mélanie's face, too, took on a pink tone. Which got me thinking I was right. That all those years ago, those two had married for love and not just a cause. That probably it was just the fear prompted by Mélanie's father that broke them apart. And probably it wasn't just Sergei who still held a place in his heart for her. I was guessing by Mélanie's actions of the evening, that she had some pretty strong feelings for him, too. Feelings she didn't want to share with anyone and maybe even tried to deny to herself. Until today, when she found out her second husband was just another cheat who used her and her first husband would do anything to protect her.

I walked over and passed Mélanie Sergei's bagged shoe.

"Here," I said. "This was in your room, so I'm returning it to you. Maybe one day, you may want to see if the guy who lost it is still a fit."

The two exchanged shy smiles. I smiled, too, happy that I may have played a small part in helping bring together two hearts that should have been together all along. Two hearts, that I knew in my own heart would eventually get their happily ever after.

As I said my goodbyes and headed for the elevator, my fingers found their way to my locket again. I couldn't say for sure that it was a Valentine miracle that brought it back to me, but I did have faith that the love tucked inside it was leading me to my own happily ever after, too.

⚜

# ACKNOWLEDGMENTS

I started this book with two goals: to write a story that unfolds within a twenty-four hour period and to have it take place in one location with few "sets." As I neared the end, I realized the story felt a bit like a play and is in part an homage to all the plays my mother took me to as a child, so I thank her and them for that inspiration.

I also thank the rest of my family and my friends and early readers for all their feedback and support. And a big thanks goes to the fab Maud L. for adding her magic flair to the French bits.

And to every reader who generously takes the time to step into the Lora Weaver world, leave a review, and help spread love of the books, a very big Merci. The same to Montréal, the city that forever lives in my heart.

# ABOUT THE AUTHOR

Katy Leen is the author of the Lora Weaver mystery novels. She credits her mom for sparking her lifelong love of stories through her own avid love of books. When she's not writing, Katy can be found listening to bookish and wellness podcasts, playing word games, reading, or hanging out with her hubby and family—always with a pup at her side and a cup of cocoa nearby.

Join Katy's *Nouvelles* newsletter where she shares more meanderings and insider info about the books:)

Pop by katyleen.com to check out the Q&A and her blog or Follow Katy at:

# ALSO BY KATY LEEN

**Series in Order**

The First Faux Pas

The Nearly Nixed Noël (holiday novella)

The Pas de Deux

The Lost Love Liaison (Valentine novella)

The Ménage à Trois

The Easter Egg Ennui (Easter novella)

The Petit-Four Score

**More Books**

The Demi-Tasse Début (prequel novella)

The Bonne Année Brouhaha (New Year's novella)

The Lora Weaver Bundle

The Lora Weaver Holiday Boxed Set

The Lora Weaver series is still growing! Pop over to my website for news about the latest books.

The series is available in print, ebook, and audiobook.

I hope you join me for more of Lora's adventures:)

Happy reading!

www.ingramcontent.com/pod-product-compliance
Lightning Source LLC
Chambersburg PA
CBHW051925220626
47052CB00003B/582